AF074517

A COWBOY'S SECRET

———————

THE MCGAVIN BROTHERS

Vicki Lewis Thompson

Ocean Dance Press

A COWBOY'S SECRET
© 2019 Vicki Lewis Thompson

ISBN: 978-1-946759-79-5

Ocean Dance Press LLC
PO Box 69901
Oro Valley, AZ 85737

All Rights Reserved. No part of this book may be used or reproduced or transmitted in any form or by any means, graphic, electronic, or mechanical, including photocopying, recording, taping, or by any information storage or retrieval system, without the written permission of the publisher except in the case of brief quotations embodied in critical articles or reviews.

This is a work of fiction. Any resemblance to actual persons, living or dead, business establishments, events, or locales is entirely coincidental.

Cover art by Kristin Bryant

Visit the author's website at
VickiLewisThompson.com

White-hot guilt stabbed him.

He had no business misleading this compassionate woman, no matter what his motives were. Time to end the charade and be truthful. "I'm not—"

"You're not worried about yourself. I know! That's the problem! I like you, Raven. I like you a whole lot. I think you must like me a little bit, too."

"Of course..." He coughed. "Of course I do." How was he supposed to be noble when she was saying exactly what he wanted to hear?

"A little while ago, I kissed you."

"I noticed."

"If you wouldn't mind, I'd like to do it again."

His voice grew thick of its own accord. "I wouldn't mind."

"It's pretty dark in here. Think you could take off your cap?"

He sent it sailing toward the counter. Truth could wait. "First kiss was yours," he murmured. "This one's mine."

Want more cowboys? Check out these other titles by Vicki Lewis Thompson

The McGavin Brothers

A Cowboy's Strength
A Cowboy's Honor
A Cowboy's Return
A Cowboy's Heart
A Cowboy's Courage
A Cowboy's Christmas
A Cowboy's Kiss
A Cowboy's Luck
A Cowboy's Charm
A Cowboy's Challenge
A Cowboy's Baby
A Cowboy's Holiday
A Cowboy's Choice
A Cowboy's Worth
A Cowboy's Destiny
A Cowboy's Secret

Thunder Mountain Brotherhood

Midnight Thunder
Thunderstruck
Rolling Like Thunder
A Cowboy Under the Mistletoe
Cowboy All Night
Cowboy After Dark
Cowboy Untamed
Cowboy Unwrapped
In the Cowboy's Arms
Say Yes to the Cowboy
Do You Take This Cowboy?

Sons of Chance
Wanted!
Ambushed!
Claimed!
Should've Been a Cowboy
Cowboy Up
Cowboys Like Us
Long Road Home
Lead Me Home
Feels Like Home
I Cross My Heart
Wild at Heart
The Heart Won't Lie
Cowboys and Angels
Riding High
Riding Hard
Riding Home
A Last Chance Christmas

__1__

Aaron polished off his beer before glancing over the latest version of his letter to Caitlin. "I think it's okay, but I can't tell anymore. My brain cells are still fried from your bachelor party." He handed it to Badger. "Take a look."

Badger scanned the paper and slid it back across the kitchen table. "You nailed it. Just needs a closin' and a signature."

"What kind of closing?"

Tilting back his chair and steepling his fingers, Badger maintained his balance with the same coordination that had made him a skilled fighter pilot. He'd been as toasted as anybody the night before, but he'd kept this Sunday evening appointment to create the letter. "Just use *Respectfully yours.* Sets the tone we're goin' for."

"Sounds old-fashioned."

"Nothin' wrong with that."

"If you say so." He scribbled the words.

"Now sign it and we're finished with that part."

"Thank God." He put his signature on the letter. Since he didn't have Badger's iron constitution, he could use some sleep. "Now we can—"

"I hate to tell you, good buddy, but you just signed your name right there."

Damn it. Sure enough, he'd automatically scribbled *Aaron Donahue.* Heaving a sigh, he reached for a blank piece of paper.

"Patience, grasshopper."

Aaron looked up and caught Badger grinning at him. "Not funny."

"Is too. Everythin' about this caper is hilarious." He paused. "You need to stay loose."

"Now you tell me."

"It's just a little play-actin', like when we dressed in drag for the squadron talent show that time."

"But we weren't trying to fool anybody with those wigs and makeup. Convincing Caitlin I'm someone else is gonna be damn near impossible."

"Me givin' her a letter from my old buddy Raven will be a good start."

"And that's the other thing. I'm not Raven anymore. That was in my other life. I haven't used that name since I was discharged. Ryker doesn't answer to Cowboy, either, except when he's with us."

"Every boy and man in Eagles Nest answers to *cowboy*. I wager this town has the highest percentage of cowboys in the—"

"Nevertheless, Ryker and I didn't hang onto our call signs like you did."

"'Cause y'all didn't get saddled with Thaddeus Livingston Calhoun the Third. And I can't help pointin' out that if you'd stuck with yours, you wouldn't be in this pickle."

"Yeah, but I didn't."

"Which is the reason we're goin' to deploy it now. I doubt Caitlin's ever heard us call you Raven. She'll think she's talkin' to a whole different person."

"That letter sure makes me sound like somebody else. I don't recognize that guy."

"Because you're not used to thinkin' of yourself as a hero."

"I'm not—"

"Wounded in action and decorated for valor. Doesn't get much more heroic unless you'd made the ultimate sacrifice. I'm personally delighted that you didn't."

"But I'm not used to talking about any of this."

"You're not talkin' about it. That's the beauty of a letter. That's how an admirer who's hesitant to lay his cards on the table in person handles this kind of situation."

"I'm only hesitant because I've got the same name as her scumbag ex."

"Exactly, and we're goin' to fix that unfortunate situation by presenting her with a genuine war hero she won't be able to resist. I get that you didn't want to put in that you were awarded a medal, but I plan to tell her."

"Please don't."

"Do you want to impress this woman or not?"

He sighed. "Yes, but—"

"Then go with the narrative. It's all true. Shot down behind enemy lines, fought off the enemy and escaped despite a broken leg."

"Only because of Ryker. I told him to leave me."

"Yes, and he's a legend in his own time, but we're focusin' on—"

"We're still not telling him?"

Badger shook his head. "Can't afford to. I'll have my hands full not tellin' Hayley. Which reminds me, we need code words."

"For what?"

"We can't talk about this on the phone if Hayley's around. Or Ryker. Or anybody, come to think of it. You can text me a code word if all's well or a different one if it's effed up. Use *Mach 3* if things are good and *tailspin* if you're scrappin' the mission."

"Okay, but I don't see how you can keep this from Hayley. Or how we'll keep Ryker from finding out. We should tell them."

"Can't. The more who know, the more likely we'll have a leak. Hayley's not a problem. Believe it or not, we go days at a time without mentionin' you."

"Yeah, okay, but we see Ryker all the time. He—"

"I don't want to burden him with a secret he can't tell April. And there's the chance he'll try to talk us out of it."

"Aha! There's the real reason you don't want to tell him."

"Because I've had experience with Cowboy in that regard. When I pretended to be

Hayley's fiancée Christmas before last, he was *not* happy that I was foolin' her parents. He told me not to." He spread his hands. "See how wrong he was?"

"Yeah, but this is different."

"Not really. Strictly speakin', I was much less truthful durin' that episode than you'll be durin' this one. You're a *genuine* hero."

Aaron smiled at the way his Southern buddy dragged out the word *genuine.* "Compared to Ryker, I'm not—"

"Don't tell me that you didn't go through hell durin' all those operations on your leg because I know better. That's hero stuff right there."

"So it wasn't a picnic, but—"

"Let's not forget the nightmares."

He shrugged. "Most returning vets have 'em. Nothing unique about that."

"And the freak sandstorm that scratched the corneas in both eyes didn't help, either. They're still sensitive."

"Not *that* sensitive. I was cleared to fly."

"With tinted goggles. Anyway, we have to exaggerate that bit so you can keep the lights low and your ball cap on."

"Badger, this isn't gonna work. She's sharp. She'll figure it out in two minutes."

"You're discountin' the sales job I'll do prior to her showin' up at your house. Southerners are natural storytellers. And charmin' on top of it."

Aaron rolled his eyes.

"If I do my job and turn you into a romantic hero, she'll want to believe. She won't be lookin' for reasons to doubt the setup. A couple of heartfelt conversations in your dimly lit livin' room and she'll start likin' you more'n a bear likes a honeycomb."

"If it gets that far, and I'm not convinced it will, she'll start liking Raven, Aaron's new roommate. How will she take it when she finds out it's been me all along?"

"She might be discombobulated at first, but by then you'll have your foot in the door. She'll realize you two get along like grits and gravy."

"I hope you're right." He scrubbed a hand over his face. "Damn it, why does her ex have to have my exact name, first *and* last?"

"I reckon his momma liked the sound of it, just like yours did."

"Guess so."

"Look at it this way. What have you got to lose?"

"My dignity."

"Tell that to someone who hasn't seen water balloons fallin' out of your dress."

* * *

Aaron brought the Cessna in for a three-point landing at Eagles Nest Airfield a little past noon the following day. He taxied over to the tie-down area reserved for Badger Air and parked next to a Piper Mohave which bore the same logo as the Cessna, a badger wearing a World War I flight helmet. Ryker had taken his beloved twin-engine Beechcraft on a run to Boise. Badger had the day off.

Working for a small commuter airline owned by his two best buddies from the Air Force was a dream job. His passengers were mostly like the couple this morning, chatty and excited about heading to Kalispell and Glacier National Park. The ride home in an empty plane had been way too quiet, though, giving him time to obsess about the letter. If Badger had followed through, Caitlin would have it by now.

She'd scheduled a morning appointment with Badger and Hayley, his fiancée, to discuss a strategy for their wedding photos. Hayley's brother Luke and his fiancée Abigail would be there, too. Logically, a double wedding required extra planning.

Somehow, despite all the folks gathering at Caitlin's studio, Badger had labeled it a perfect opportunity to give her the letter. Privately. That was Badger, always bucking the odds.

He'd promised not to reveal their scheme to anyone until after the wedding, which was in six short days. By then their identity switch would have succeeded brilliantly or failed miserably. Either way, it would be out in the open. Secrets didn't last long in a small town.

As Aaron walked into the terminal, Badger pushed open the glass front door. His quick smile and thumbs up signaled he'd launched the mission. Aaron's stomach bottomed out.

"Figured you'd have landed by now." Badger nudged back the brim of his Stetson. He'd retained his Georgia accent, but he'd adopted the clothes and mannerisms of a Montana cowboy.

He glanced around. "Good deal. Nobody's here. I have excellent news. She was moved by your letter and she's willin' to meet with you. Eager to meet you, in fact. I did a damned good job, if I do say so."

"When?"

"Tonight. At your house, like we discussed."

"Yikes."

"That's what you and I agreed on."

"I know. I'm just..." *Not ready.* "If she's coming to the house to meet Raven, where am I supposed to be?"

"You're flyin' to Casper tonight and won't be back until tomorrow so Raven has the house to himself. If all goes well, we'll send you off somewhere the next night, too." Badger peered at him. "You look a little green around the gills."

"I honestly didn't think you'd have a chance to give her the letter."

"Turned out to be easy. Hayley rushed off for a girls-only lunch with her mom. Delilah had a run-in with a skunk early this mornin' so Luke and Abigail headed back home to give her another bath. I hung back, claiming I had a few more questions for Caitlin. Mission accomplished."

Aaron gulped. He'd flown with Badger in combat without breaking a sweat. He was sweating, now. "You know what? This is crazy. Let's forget it."

"Forget it? What are you talkin' 'bout?"

"Look, you put a lot of effort into this and I appreciate it more than I can say, but—"

"All righty, then." Badger shrugged. "I'll text her and say Raven chickened out."

"Fine with me."

"Kinda funny, though, a raven chickening out." He grinned. *"Caw-caw-caw."* Then he flapped his elbows. *"Cluck-cluck-cluck."*

"Yeah, yeah, go ahead. I deserve it. I should have nixed this wacko plan from the get-go. Don't know what I was thinking."

"You were thinkin' it's the only way around your problem. Which it is."

"Or I could just accept the fact that she won't date me."

"Are you goin' to?"

Aaron met his gaze. "Probably not."

"That's what I thought you said the first time we explored this option."

"I know, but now that it's actually—"

"You'll be fine. The run-through last night was impressive."

"So you said."

"When you put on a ball cap instead of your Stetson, you look like Raven, my old wingman. You act more like him, too. The guy I flew with was bold. Inventive. Always doin' the unexpected. A *raven*."

Aaron took a deep breath.

"The scruff helps the disguise, too. Makes you look edgy. I'd forgotten you shave twice a day. It's only noon and you already have some bristle goin' on."

"And cold feet."

"Then bail out, compadre. There's always the Internet for findin' women."

"Doesn't appeal to me."

"But Caitlin does?"

"Yes, damn it."

"Then you'd better unleash your inner jet jockey, good buddy. It's show time."

2

Twilight settled gently over Eagles Nest, triggering dusk-to-dawn porch lights in the cozy neighborhood where Aaron lived. A bracing wave of cold air scented with the aroma of a juniper fire greeted Caitlin as she stepped out of her trusty old Cherokee.

The number on the rural mailbox by the curb matched the one Badger had given her, and the dark green Craftsman-style house fit his description. Lights in the window were muted, but she'd been told to expect that.

Anticipation jacked up her pulse. Who could resist getting to know a shy war hero who'd admired her from afar? Although Raven's letter hadn't said so, Badger had confided that the guy had been decorated for bravery. She had a soft spot for vets.

Taking the walkway to the porch, she reached for her phone to record the mosaic of fall leaves on the dry grass. Then she tucked it back in her jacket pocket. Much as she loved autumn colors, she wasn't here to take pictures.

She climbed the porch steps as a breeze caught red and yellow leaves and sent them skittering across the white floorboards to gather under a couple of rattan chairs. She rang the doorbell.

A broad-shouldered man who was likely six-two or three opened the door. He'd tugged his ball cap down so it shaded his eyes. Badger had said his buddy had been caught in a sandstorm that had scratched the corneas in both eyes.

"Raven?" She held out her hand.

"Yes." His voice was husky as he clasped her hand in a firm grip. Maybe the sandstorm had affected his throat, too. He released her hand and stepped back. "Please come in. Thanks for doing this."

"I'm happy to meet with you. I'm glad you sent word through Badger. You must be keeping a low profile because I didn't know another member of Ryker and Badger's squadron was in town."

"A *very* low profile." He sounded slightly amused. "Can I take your jacket?"

"Sure." She slipped out of it and handed it over.

When he walked the short distance to the coat tree by the door, he favored his right leg.

"Do you still have pain from your injury?"

"Not too much anymore. We can talk over there, if that's okay." He gestured toward a pair of easy chairs that faced the fireplace. Two bottles of beer sat on a table between the chairs and the soft glow of a fire struck a welcoming note in the dim room.

"Looks perfect. I love the built-in bookshelves by the fireplace. And all the books. Aaron must be quite a reader."

"Yep."

She wandered over to the shelf on the left. "Ooo, he has some Dick Francis I haven't read."

"I'm sure he'd loan 'em to you."

"I'll ask next time I see him."

"Take a couple now. He won't mind."

She ran a finger over the spines of the books. Dust jackets still on. Chronological order. "Maybe not, but I'll ask, first. This could be the complete set. Clearly he treasures his books." She gestured to the chairs. "Does it matter where I sit?"

"Nope." He cleared his throat. "I didn't drink from either bottle."

Clearing his throat hadn't changed the gravelly texture of his voice. If anything, it was more pronounced. He could be self-conscious about that, too. She chose the nearest chair. "McGavin's Pale Ale. My new favorite."

"Mine, too."

"I only mentioned your injury because April is a terrific massage therapist. I go to her all the time." Picking up her beer, she took a sip. "Then again, maybe Ryker's already set you up with her."

"No, he…uh…doesn't know I'm here."

"He doesn't?" She stared at him. "Why not?"

"I need to work on some things. Badger and Aaron get that, but Ryker…"

"I think he'd get it, too."

"Maybe. But he might not go along with… my methods." A ripple in his voice sounded like he might have swallowed laughter.

But that made no sense. "What methods?"

"They're...unconventional." He ducked his head, but didn't move fast enough. Firelight picked up the quick flash of a smile.

She was encouraged by that smile. Despite what he'd been through, he'd held onto his sense of humor. The contrast of white teeth against his dark bristle was attractive. Rakish, even. "I guess I shouldn't mention this meeting to anyone."

"I'd appreciate that."

"Then I won't." The plot thickened. And she was a sucker for intrigue. "But I'm curious about what you're doing that Ryker wouldn't go along with."

"Psychological experiment." He took a swallow of his beer. "May not work."

"Hey, I'm from SoCal, the land of experimental psychology. Maybe I can help."

"Explaining would ruin it."

"Is my being here part of it?"

"In a way."

"Wow. This is more complicated than I thought. I'm fascinated, though."

He nodded. "That's good news."

"Will you explain it to me when the experiment's over?"

"Definitely."

"Can you tell me when that will be?"

"Friday."

"That's not very much time."

"No."

"If it helps the cause, I have some time the next three evenings."

"It would help."

The experiment will be over by Friday. She gazed at him. "I'll bet I've figured it out. Badger wants you to attend his wedding on Saturday and he thinks a few conversations with me beforehand will help you gear up for it."

He glanced away.

"Did I guess it?"

"Well..."

"Never mind. If that's the plan, it's fine. But even if talking with me is helpful, I can't be your support person during the wedding. I'll be very busy."

"No problem."

"Well, good." She took another swallow of her beer. "So here we are. What would you like to talk about?"

"You."

"Could you be more specific?"

"Your work. How you got started."

"That's an easy one. I had a toy camera when I was a toddler. By the time I was three, I was driving my parents nuts begging for one that took real pictures. They tell me I was relentless, but I like to think I was sweet about it."

That cute little smile reappeared. "Nothing wrong with asking for what you want."

"Absolutely." Right now, she wanted to see his whole face instead of only the bottom half. But in addition to protecting his eyes, the hat might give him a sense of security. She didn't want to threaten that. "What else would you like to know?"

Instead of looking at her, he stared at the beer bottle he cradled in both hands. He had a scar on the back of one. "So you grew up in California?"

"All over." She took another drink. "My brother and I were Navy brats."

"Yeah?"

"My dad was career military. My brother only served four years, said that was enough excitement to last him."

"I get that."

"I'm sure you do. Anyway, my parents ended up in San Diego, the last place Dad was stationed before he retired. Now Dennis is there, too."

"Why not you?"

"Competition is stiff in SoCal and I was tired of fighting for my place in that environment. The beach is awesome, but the traffic isn't. I longed for fewer people and four distinct seasons. Fall is a special favorite of mine."

"I like it, too."

"Especially when the leaves turn."

"Yeah. That's nice."

"You have some awesome leaves in your yard and on your porch. I almost stopped to take pictures."

"You should do that tomorrow night."

"Okay, I will. Maybe I'll bring a real camera."

"Excellent." He gave her a quick glance before looking away again. "So that's why you're here? Leaves and less people?"

She laughed. "Partly. The main reason is—I love cowboys."

"Oh?"

"As photographic subjects, I mean. The American cowboy as a symbol of chivalry is one worth preserving. Living here, I have plenty of opportunities to shoot cowboys. But I'm not...it's not as if I have a thing for..."

"Not attracted to the Stetson?"

"I'm more interested in what's in a guy's head than what's on it. Although you hardly see anybody around here, male or female, who isn't wearing a cowboy hat."

"True."

"I would be surprised if Aaron hasn't already bought you one."

"He has."

"But you're clinging to your ball cap, instead?"

"I'm used to it." He tugged on the curved bill.

"It does a good job of shading your eyes, better than a Stetson would, I think, so you're probably wise to stick with it until your eyes heal."

"Right." He took a mouthful of beer.

"I'm curious about your name."

"Oh?"

"Is it your real one?"

3

He choked on his beer and almost spewed it everywhere. Setting the bottle on the small table between them, he leaned forward and coughed several times before straightening and taking a deep breath.

"Better?"

"Yes. Sorry."

"Was that the wrong thing to ask?"

Yes. "No." Choking had roughened his voice, which was a big help. Keeping that rasp going had turned into a major challenge. "It's the name my squadron gave me."

"Like Badger?"

"Exactly."

"So you use it in place of your given name?"

"For now." Except for the choking episode, responses were sliding off his tongue and he hadn't lied yet. Badger would be proud of him.

"You must like it."

"I do."

"Does it have significance? Or is it just because you have black hair?"

How did she know that? Oh, yeah, his beard. And his hair below the back of the cap. "Partly the hair. And I can...repair things using...random stuff." He'd have a sore throat for real if he kept this up much longer. "Ravens are inventive."

She studied him. "It's a useful trait."

"It's handy." *Like now.* She was looking too closely, though, examining him with her perceptive blue gaze. "I'd better tend the fire." Leaving the chair, he exaggerated his limp slightly as he moved over to the hearth. "What does your name mean?"

She chuckled. "Pure. I looked it up when I was about sixteen. I asked my mom if my name meant I was supposed to be a virgin the rest of my life."

"What'd she say?"

"She thought it meant pure of heart, not celibate. I was incredibly relieved, especially since I'd just seen a movie where Brad Pitt was shirtless."

He smiled and continued rearranging the logs on the fire. "Angelina Jolie was my wake-up call."

"I kind of hated that they couldn't make a go of it."

"Celebrity's tough duty." Adjusting the brim of his hat for maximum shadow, he returned to his chair.

"It sure is. I'd much rather be behind the camera than in front of it."

"Is that why I didn't see any pictures of you on the town's website?"

"I know it's crazy, but I don't like having my picture taken. I've been told I should have a head shot, at least, on my website."

"You should."

"I suppose I will, eventually. It's not a priority."

He'd love to try capturing the essence of her in a picture. He'd take it while she was working, when her light brown hair was coming out of her braids and her blue eyes were shining with the challenge of getting the perfect shot.

He couldn't believe she was here, sitting beside him. She'd dressed up for this meeting, a sweet gesture. He'd never seen that soft blue sweater before, or her hair down and curling over her shoulders. She'd worn light pink lipstick and a little eye makeup. For him. No, for Raven.

She was much quieter tonight. Usually she was in constant motion, chatting with everyone as she dashed around, alternating between her video and her still cameras.

Not tonight. He had her all to himself and he liked her more with every minute they spent together. She'd refused to borrow any of his prized set of Dick Francis books without asking. Not that she needed extra points since he was already hooked, but she'd impressed him with that decision.

Too bad they couldn't compare notes on those books. At least not yet. In the meantime, he had so much else he wanted to know about her. "What kind of movies do you like?"

"Ones with happy endings. I'm not into the tragic stories where they all die in the end."

Right answer. "Me, either. When I watch, that is." *Don't forget your eye problems, doofus.*

"I guess you would have to take a break from movies. I'll bet you can't read any of these fabulous books Aaron has, either." She gazed at him. "Was it all worth it?"

He'd asked himself the question many times. Now that he was back and more-or-less in one piece, he could finally answer. "Yes. Good cause, made lifelong friends. And…nothing like flying faster than sound." Then again, he'd never held Caitlin in his arms. That might beat the thrill of streaking across the sky at Mach 3.

"I can't imagine being in combat."

"I thought I knew what I was getting into, but…" He took another drink and cleared his throat.

"Intense?"

"It's not a video game."

"But you made it home."

"Yeah." A familiar pain tightened his chest. "Took a toll on my mom."

"Any siblings?"

"No. She's alone. She went through hell while I was gone. Never let on." He didn't have to fake the catch in his throat. Talking about his mom choked him up. She was far braver than he'd ever been.

"Does she live near Eagles Nest?"

"Not yet." He took a breath. "I'm working on it. She's owned her house a long time."

"Where?"

"Ohio. It's nice. Familiar. But Ryker showed me pictures of Eagles Nest and I loved it on sight. Mom's coming out next month to visit."

"It's a friendly town. You may not have had much chance to—"

"Very friendly." He cut her off before she said something he'd have to confirm or deny. "Whoever sees your Fourth of July video gets that."

"I like how it turned out. Has your mom seen it?"

"It convinced her to come."

"Aww. I'm gratified to hear that."

"Aleck's bagpipes helped, too. She loves bagpipes."

"Hey, that reminds me. Have you heard Badger play?"

"Not yet." He and Ryker figured they deserved to hear a few notes since they'd been listening to Badger rave about his lessons for weeks. But the guy was going for a big reveal on Saturday. He'd found a secret practice location that even Hayley didn't know about.

"Aleck claims he's getting good, but I guess he won't go public until the wedding."

"That's what he says."

"Another reason why you need to be there. He's getting married and making his musical debut on the bagpipes." She finished off her beer.

"Oh, I'll be there."

"Whether your experiment works or not?"

"I wouldn't miss it for anything." Not even the total humiliation he'd face if she shot him down when she learned the truth.

"That's nice, Raven. I'm glad you feel that way."

"He's my friend." He glanced at her empty bottle. "Can I get you another beer?"

"Better not. The senior portraits I shot over the weekend need retouching and I promised to have them ready tomorrow."

"I took you away from your work."

"Not a problem." She stood. "I've enjoyed this."

Yes! He got out of his chair. "So have I. I'll fetch your jacket." He averted his face and started toward the coat tree because the big ol' grin threatening to break through might give him away.

She followed him over. "Easing back into civilian life might seem like a challenge at first, but you picked the right town. And a good roommate. Aaron seems like a very nice guy."

"He's awesome." Not easy to say with a straight face. Fortunately, the area by the door was darker than over by the fire. He unhooked her jacket from the coat tree.

"I'm sure he is. I get the impression he'd like to hang out with me, which is why I told him the thing about my ex-boyfriend's name right away. Did he mention that?"

The intel had carved permanent grooves in his brain, but Raven wouldn't be nearly as dialed in. "You'd better refresh my memory." He held her jacket for her.

"I was serious about a guy in San Diego until he cheated on me."

He'd winced the first time she'd told him and he did it again. How could anyone cheat on Caitlin? The guy had to be terminally dumb. "I'm sorry."

"I won't lie. It was painful. Didn't see it coming." Slipping her arms into her jacket sleeves caused her hair to sway gently, releasing a sweet fragrance.

The scent drew him closer. With great effort, he took a step back. "It's no fun to be blindsided."

"No fun at all." She flipped her hair over the jacket collar and turned to face him. "But here's the part that's kind of weird, but also sad. My ex's name is Aaron Donahue."

"Ah. That rings a bell." More like a large Chinese gong. "Aaron did mention it."

She began buttoning her jacket. "Naturally, when I met the Eagles Nest Aaron, I had a visceral negative reaction."

"Naturally."

"I even said something stupid like *I could never trust you.* Then I caught myself and apologized. I told him the problem. He said he understood, but he looked unhappy. As well he would be. It's not his fault that a total jerk has his name."

"Nope."

"Then tonight I find out he has an entire collection of Dick Francis, an author I *love*. My ex only read fitness magazines." She shoved her hands in her pockets. "He was proud of his muscles. Bragged about how much he could bench-press. Loser."

"Aaron never brags about his muscles."

"Of course not. He's a decent human being." She gazed at him. "So are you, Raven. I guess you'd have to be or Aaron wouldn't have invited you to room with him and Badger wouldn't be asking me to help acclimate you before the ceremony this weekend. I'm sure it'll be wild."

"Well, it's Badger's wedding, after all."

She laughed. "Yes, there's that. The guy can't do anything without making a production of it. The bagpipes are an interesting twist, but the event was always going to be epic." She took a breath. "I'd better head home."

"Thanks for coming."

"My pleasure. So, same time tomorrow night?"

"Works for me if it works for you."

"It does. Will Aaron be here?"

"Uh, no, he's flying to Casper."

"Again?"

Damn. "No, you're right. That's where he is tonight. He'll be in Kalispell tomorrow night."

"Okay. I thought if he was here, I could ask about the books. But I could call him." She pulled out her phone. "What's his number?"

Aaron reeled it off.

"Wow, you knew it without looking at your phone."

Uh-oh. "For some reason his stuck in my head."

"That's amazing. I don't know anybody's number anymore now that they're all in my list of contacts. Would you mind giving me your number, too?"

Oh, geez. "Um, I would, but...I think it's smart to switch from the Ohio area code to the Montana one, so I'm—"

"In transition. That's okay. I can get it later. You have mine, right?"

"I do." His heartbeat gradually returned to normal.

Reaching over, she gave his forearm a squeeze. "See you tomorrow night."

"See you then."

He stayed very still until she started her Jeep and drove away. Then he let out a whoop and busted some moves. He'd messed up a little at the end, but he'd avoided total disaster. Bottom line— he'd done it.

He texted Badger. *Mach 3.*

Badger called him back. "You actually pulled it off?"

"You didn't think I would?"

"I gave you a forty-percent chance, but I didn't want to say it and destroy what little confidence you had in the mission."

"Glad I beat the odds, then. Why did you call me back? Where's Hayley?"

"In the shower. So are you saying Caitlin bought the whole setup?"

"Evidently."

"Damn, I'm good."

"I almost screwed up at the end. She asked for Aaron's phone number and was surprised that I knew it without looking it up."

"No kiddin'. I barely know my own, let alone yours. Why'd she want it?"

"She's a Dick Francis fan and wants to ask me about borrowing some books."

"See there? Already you have Dick Francis in common. I predict you'll keep uncoverin' gems like that."

"Then she asked for my number, meaning Raven's."

"How'd you wiggle out of that?"

"I told her it made sense to switch from an Ohio area code to a Montana one and I implied that chore was on my to-do list."

"Quick thinkin'."

"Appreciate the compliment. Oh, and she's coming back tomorrow night, same time. I said Aaron will be in Kalispell. She's mentioned that she's free the next two nights after that, so we'll have to figure out where Aaron's off to so it makes sense."

"No problemo."

"I'm thinking maybe I'll shave for the next—"

"Hold the phone, Einstein."

"I feel like a derelict when I don't shave."

"Have you got grits for brains?"

"The scruff is not my style."

"It's Raven's style. Stick with it."

"It's only the bottom half of my face. Batman shows the bottom half of his face and nobody recognizes Bruce Wayne."

"I hate to break it to you, hotshot, but that's a movie. It's not real. And Caitlin's a photographer. She notices details. Don't shave."

"But I hate feeling like—"

"Hayley's out of the shower. Gotta go. Don't shave." Badger disconnected.

Aaron rubbed his prickly jaw. Maybe if he turned off one of the lamps...

4

The following afternoon, Caitlin kept an eye on the time as she finished up a Wild Creek photo shoot with two ENHS seniors. A year ago, she'd struck a deal with Kendra to use the ranch for outdoor portrait work, the bulk of which would be senior portraits.

The concept was insanely successful, providing a great opportunity for Caitlin and another revenue stream for Kendra, plus extra exposure for her stable. The high school kids had been overjoyed with the concept.

Foreman Jim Underwood seemed to get a kick out of the teenagers and always made sure he was on hand to help. The two girls for today's shoot had chosen Winston, a flashy butterscotch Paint, and Strawberry, a gentle roan, to step into the limelight with them. The horses had lapped up the extra attention, especially Winston, the most extroverted horse Caitlin had ever met.

Senior portraits created a rush of business this month because the weather was perfect for outdoor shots. She was determined to stay ahead of the game because the wedding would suck up so much of her weekend.

Technically she didn't have the bandwidth to spend time with Raven right now. But she wanted to. He was at a critical juncture in his life and she wanted to help.

Besides, he was sweet and...yeah, attractive. His understated sexiness came through, despite the ball cap and the dim lights. Or maybe because of them. A man of mystery. Sharing a beer and conversation with him wasn't a chore.

After the girls left, she thanked Jim for his part in the photo shoot and walked up to the main house to let Kendra know she'd finished. The girls hadn't chosen to use the long front porch of the massive log house, but Caitlin loved working with its rustic appeal, too.

She'd posed other teen clients in the rockers or on the steps. The sturdy railing was a multipurpose prop for casual leaning. Some kids had opted to climb up and stand on it.

Tapping on the carved wooden door, she opened it a crack. "Kendra? You in there?"

"Sure am. Talking to Ryker. Come join us."

So that was who'd arrived in the familiar-looking truck parked beside hers. After last night, she'd just as soon not interact with him and risk letting something slip. It still seemed odd that Badger and Aaron had kept him in the dark about Raven.

Yes, Ryker's military bearing intimidated a lot of people, but Aaron and Badger were his squadron buddies. Strange that they'd left him out of the loop this week.

He was sitting at the table drinking coffee with his mom when Caitlin walked in. He got to his feet. "Hey, Caitlin. Good to see you. Can I get you a cup?"

"I'm afraid I can't stay long." She walked over and slid into the chair he pulled out for her. "Thanks. How are you?"

"Good. Lots of last-minute wedding stuff, but that's typical."

She smiled. "Always." She turned to Kendra. "Three ENHS boys would like to come out tomorrow afternoon, same time frame. Will that work?"

"Absolutely. I meant to tell you that Faith and I shifted weekday riding lessons to morning and early afternoon to give you the run of the place after school lets out. We'll keep that schedule until the weather changes."

"Thanks. Good to know."

"I was watching out the window," Ryker said. "Those girls had a blast."

"So did I. They were a little self-conscious at first, but once I coaxed them into having fun with it, we had a great time."

"April and I were looking at our album last night and everyone's relaxed and happy, even in the posed shots. You're great at putting people at ease."

"That's nice to hear. And Saturday we get to do it all again."

"Yes, ma'am. Should be...interesting."

"You mean because of Badger on the bagpipes?"

"I'm not worried about Badger. If he commits to something he does it and does it right. It's Delilah I'm concerned about."

"I heard about the skunk incident when Luke and Abigail met with me yesterday, but they had some special stuff and said the stink would be gone by this weekend."

"I don't care how she smells. Well, I do, but you're right. They're on top of it. I just don't like putting her in charge of four valuable rings. It has me spooked."

Kendra laughed. "Pot, meet kettle. Your wedding was a disaster waiting to happen. Wrangling one cute little doggie pales in comparison to what you put us through, my darling son."

"I can't argue with that, but those meteorite wedding rings Badger bought cost a fortune and—"

"He likely has them insured."

"But they're unique, one-of-a-kind." He heaved a sigh. "I wish they'd let me and Wes take charge of the rings. I understand they want Delilah in the wedding, but she could be the flower dog."

"The ring-bearer is a more significant role," Caitlin said. "They'll be tied to her collar. Easier to do that than decorate her with flowers."

"Virginia's determined to get some kind of outfit on her, though. Last I heard it was a doggie tux. Delilah won't like that."

"You never know. She might." Kendra regarded him with fondness. "Just because you hate them doesn't mean everybody does."

"I'm betting Delilah will be fine." Caitlin pushed back her chair.

"I hope you're right. Anyway, I'd better head out, too." He stood and plucked his hat from the table.

"I'm right behind you." Caitlin got up.

"Thanks for the coffee, Mom." Ryker settled his hat on his head as he walked to the front door, opened it and waited for Caitlin. "I'll walk you out."

"Okay." She gave him a smile. Kendra's boys had such lovely manners.

After he closed the door, he followed her down the steps. "I'd like to ask you about something."

"Sure."

"This has been on my mind for some time. I told myself not to get involved, but Aaron's my friend, so I'd like to say my piece."

Uh-oh. "About what?"

"He admires you."

"I'm aware of that, but—"

"I know he has the same name as your ex, which is unfortunate because my buddy's a great guy. Good pilot, good soldier, good friend."

"I believe you."

"He'd hate that I'm speaking up for him, but…is there any chance you can overlook the name thing?"

She took a deep breath. "I wish I could. Tell me, have you ever had a bad reaction to someone because their name had a lousy association?"

He paused beside her Jeep and nudged back his hat. "I have, in fact. If April and I have kids, she's lobbied for a girl's name she loves, but it's the same as a former commanding officer who is the meanest, most vindictive woman I've ever known. Our daughter can't have that name."

"There's my problem in a nutshell."

"But you're over this guy, right?"

"I'm *so* over him."

"How long has it been?"

"Almost two years."

"That's a decent amount of time. Maybe, in another few months, you'll be able to—"

"When was the last time you dealt with your mean and vindictive commanding officer?"

"She was transferred while I was still over there, so it's been about…five years."

"Five years since you laid eyes on this woman, and you still associate her name with negative emotions?"

"Yes, ma'am." He grimaced. "I get your point. I do. I just wish…" He shook his head. "Never mind." He opened the driver's door for her. "It's just Aaron's bad luck. Nothing to be done."

"I'm afraid that's true. Just one of those dumb coincidences." She climbed in but left the door open. She gazed up at him. "I'm sorry."

"Don't give it another thought. See you Friday afternoon if not before." He touched two fingers to the brim of his hat and walked over to his truck.

Closing the door, she fastened her seat belt and started her Jeep. *Don't give it another thought.* Too bad she couldn't shut off her brain that easily. Flick of a switch. Wouldn't that be nice?

She drove into town, turned down the alley that ran behind the row of buildings on Main Street, and parked behind the one she'd claimed as her studio and living space. The setup—commercial venture on the first floor and owner's apartment on the second—mimicked several other businesses in this block.

The town dated back to an era when shopkeepers living above their establishments had been the norm. In Eagles Nest, it still was, and she loved the vintage atmosphere.

After downloading her afternoon's work to her computer, she composed a joint email to the three seniors confirming tomorrow's photo shoot. She started to put away her camera equipment and paused. Those autumn leaves in Aaron's yard wouldn't be there forever and Raven had invited her to take some pictures.

She left her favorite digital camera on the desk where she wouldn't forget it and hurried up the stairway to take a quick shower. But first she'd call Aaron about the books.

She picked up her phone and scrolled through her contacts. She'd deleted her ex long ago. Didn't matter. A creepy deja-vu vibe hit her when she tapped on Aaron's listing.

Evidently a shared love of Dick Francis wasn't enough to override the ick clinging to her cheating bastard's name. Borrowing the books would create a connection. Could it get awkward?

Maybe she shouldn't borrow them, after all. But a couple were ones she'd never been able to find, new or used. Raven might have already said something to Aaron. Okay, it was a loan of books between friends. She was way overthinking it.

He might not even be available to answer her call since he was flying to Kalispell tonight. She'd leave a voice message and he could reply to it. Neat and tidy. She made the call.

"Hello."

"Oh! Hi, Aaron. It's Caitlin. I didn't think you'd answer. Aren't you flying to Kalispell tonight?"

"Haven't left yet. Raven told me you'd like to borrow some Dick Francis books."

"I would, but they're in such pristine condition that I'm hesitant."

"Gonna slop coffee on 'em? Dog-ear the pages?"

"*No!* I would never—"

"Kidding." His soft laughter sounded...nice. "You're a perfectionist with your photography. I think I can trust you with my books."

"Thank you. I'll be very—you know what? I shouldn't take them now. I'm crazy busy with the senior portraits, the wedding, and...well, helping Raven. I won't have time to read."

"Go ahead and take them, anyway, since you'll be coming over tonight. Keep them until you're done. It's great to know someone else in town is a fan."

"Same here. What got you started reading him?"

"The horses. Then I found out about his military service and felt a kinship there. But mostly it was my love of horses. It's one reason I was so eager to move here once Cowb—I mean, Ryker—started talking about Eagles Nest."

"Do you ride a lot?"

"Every chance I get. Wild Creek has some amazing trails."

"They do. And this weather is perfect, but I won't get any time to go until after the wedding."

"Yeah, we'll all have more time after this weekend." He paused.

Uh-oh. Was he about to suggest they go riding? "Speaking of time, I should—"

"Right. Me, too. And thanks for working with Raven when you're so crunched."

She exhaled. "I'm happy to do it. He's a sweetheart. I'm glad he has you and Badger in his corner."

"And now you."

"Yes, definitely me. Anyway, we both need to get going. Thanks for being so generous with your books. I promise I'll—"

"No promises necessary. Like I said, I'm not worried. I know they're in good hands."

"They are. Have a safe flight to Kalispell."

"I will. See you Friday night for the rehearsal."

"See you then. 'Bye..." She trailed off, unwilling to say his name and risk interrupting the flow of positive energy.

"'Bye, Caitlin." He disconnected.

She stared at the phone. Had he said her name on purpose? Well, he could do that all he wanted, but she didn't have to reciprocate. People had conversations all the time without using names.

He had a *very* nice voice, though. Deep and gentle, it was super easy on the ears. She'd talked with him in person a few times, but this was their first contact by phone. It focused her attention, emphasizing texture and timbre in a way that face-to-face conversations wouldn't.

She'd enjoyed his soft, intimate laugh when he'd teased her about messing up his books. The sound of it would stay with her for a while. It sent little shivers up her spine and made her smile. Maybe there was hope for a friendship after all. She'd just avoid saying his name.

5

Aaron sighed as he put down his phone and started making himself some dinner. For a moment, she'd been into him. He'd debated inviting her to go riding after the wedding was over. Had she sensed it? Seemed likely judging from the way she'd jumped into the conversation to deflect that potential move.

This name thing was such a stupid handicap. He chafed under the disguise Badger had dreamed up. Instead he longed to face Caitlin as himself, a confident guy with the strength of character to obliterate this damned obstacle.

Badger would tell him it was too soon. *I don't reckon a mutual love of Dick Francis is enough to light her fire. You need to keep goin', keep learnin' more about her and vice-versa.*

Badger would be right. Aaron rubbed a hand over his jaw. Okay, he'd play the damaged vet again tonight, but he'd do it with a fresh shave.

An hour later, he'd eaten, shaved and built a small fire when Caitlin tapped on his front door. He opened it a few inches and stayed back. A sunset glow lit the sky and might reveal too much, especially now that his bristle was gone. "Gonna take some pictures of the leaves?" He was getting better at sounding different without straining his vocal cords.

"I was planning on it. Could you put on sunglasses and come out? Or do you need to keep an eye on the fire?"

"It'll be okay for a while." Sunglasses plus the ball cap should be enough to maintain the secrecy. He'd go with it. After all, that's what Hollywood stars used.

"You might want to put on a sweatshirt or something. The temperature's dropped quite a bit."

"Okay. Be right there." Grabbing his flight jacket from the coat tree by the door, he shoved his arms into the sleeves and was almost out the door before he remembered to take off his name tag. Sticking it in the pocket of his jeans, he put on his aviators and stepped out on the porch.

His eye sensitivity was a real thing, just not as bad as he'd led her to believe. He wore his shades even with a Stetson, except during Ryker's outdoor wedding last April, when they'd seemed inappropriate.

Shades in place, ball cap tugged down, he stepped out on the porch.

Caitlin lay on her stomach on the dry grass while she aimed her camera across the crazy quilt of leaves littering the yard. She took several shots, then rolled to her back and focused on the leaves overhead. Watching her as she recorded the world around her was always a treat.

Hopping to her feet, she brushed off the leaves and looped the camera strap over her head bandolier-style so the camera rested on her hip. Then she turned toward the porch. "There you are." She spread out her arms. "Glorious."

"Uh-huh." Yes, she certainly was. A couple of red leaves had tangled in her hair, making her look like a wood sprite.

"I've got what I need in the yard." She came up the walk toward him. "I want to take a few shots of the leaves on the porch."

He started down the steps. "Then I'll get out of your—"

"You shaved." Her gaze lit with approval. "Wow. What a big change."

"Really?" *Yikes.*

"You look like a different person without the scruff."

He started to sweat. "I do?"

"When you were unshaven, it was as if you were in hiding."

Yep, right on the first try.

"But without the scruff, I see a man who's in the process of opening himself to what life has to offer."

"Oh." *Whew.* "Maybe I am."

"That's very good news, Raven." She smiled as if he'd given her a gift. She put her whole face into it. Her eyes sparkled, her cheeks glowed and her generous mouth curved with infectious joy.

He couldn't help smiling back. "You're beautiful." The murmured words had tumbled out, unbidden.

Her eyes grew wide and her lips parted in surprise.

Too much, too soon. "Sorry." He ducked his head and cleared his throat to resume his new way of speaking. "That was uncalled for."

"Please don't apologize."

He glanced up and met her warm gaze. "But—"

"You caught me off guard, but what woman doesn't love being told she's beautiful? It's even better when a man says it like you did, with conviction."

"Because it's true."

"Thank you."

"Especially..." He coughed to roughen his voice even more. "Especially with leaves in your hair."

"I picked up some leaves?" She lifted her hands to her hair and plucked one of them loose. "So I did. Nature girl, that's me."

"There's one more. Hold still." He combed his fingers through the silky strands and pulled it free. "Here you go. A souvenir."

"Pretty." She took the leaf by its stem and added it to the other one. Then she put her hand on his shoulder and rose on her toes.

Surely she wasn't going to...*yes, she was...*

Dipping her head under the brim of his cap, she brushed a kiss over his mouth. "Thank you."

He swallowed and fisted his hands at his sides. "Welcome." *Breathe, dude.*

Stepping back, she glanced at the sky. "I'd better capture the leaves on the porch before the light's gone."

He moved aside so she could slip past him on the narrow walkway. "By...by all means." Sheesh, he couldn't seem to get enough air. Anyone would think he'd never been kissed before. "I'll wait here."

"I won't be long." She lifted her camera strap over her head as she headed toward the porch. "I'm looking forward to enjoying another fire and a bottle of McGavin's Pale Ale."

Good thing she wanted to take some more pictures. Gave him time to collect himself. Hands in his jacket pockets, he took several restorative breaths as she twirled around the porch getting various angles on the leaves.

She moved lightly and effortlessly, almost dancing in her endless pursuit of beauty. She was tuned in to her environment, likely tuned in to him, too.

And she'd kissed him. Well, she'd kissed Raven. How should he interpret that? His body had reacted instantly. He'd locked down his response, but the strength of it served as a warning. His craving simmered just below the surface.

Why had she kissed him? Was it a friendly gesture that meant nothing more than a handshake? Or was it an attempt to change the dynamic between them to something more personal? He had no idea. Might be good to talk about it and diffuse the situation.

"Is it okay if I take a picture of you?"

Uh-oh. "I'd really—"

"The sunset's all orangey behind you. Very atmospheric. I want you to see what I see. Then I'll delete it if you want me to."

"All right. What should I—"

"Just stand there." She came down the steps, taking shot after shot as she drew closer. About three feet away, she stopped. "Nice."

"I doubt it."

She grinned. "The way you were standing in the fading light in your flight jacket and aviators, you stirred up some *Top Gun* fantasies."

He groaned.

"I know, I know. My brother flew with the Navy and you should hear his rant on the movie. I thought I was past my obsession with fighter pilots, but evidently I'm not totally over it."

Not the most terrible news he'd ever heard. "Ready to go in?"

"You bet. The light's gone, anyway." Turning, she made her way back to the porch. "I talked to Aaron earlier about the books."

"I know." He took the steps two at a time so he could open the door for her.

"Raven! Your leg!"

Damn. Forgot. "It's not bad today. Isn't bothering me much." He ushered her through the door.

"Does the weather make a difference?"

"It does." That much was true. "I can predict rain." But his leg barely hurt at all anymore, even when it rained. Just twinges.

"I'm humbled by the sacrifices made by our military personnel. Those of us who've stayed home, comfy and secure, owe you so much."

"Thank you." He followed her in and closed the door. "It wasn't all sacrifice. I made friends and learned to fly." Stripping his conversation of extraneous words minimized the strain on his vocal cords.

"Are you hoping to fly for Badger Air?" She took her camera over to the easy chair she'd used the night before and laid it on the seat. "Once you're up to it, of course."

"Yes." He'd better be up to it tomorrow, since he was heading to Boise to pick up some folks who'd been invited to the wedding. Badger was covering the cost of flying in any guests who lived within a five-hundred-mile radius of Eagles Nest.

"That's great. I'm sure Badger and Ryker can find a place for you." She shrugged out of her jacket.

"Hope so." He tucked his aviators in his pocket. "I'll take that." He hung her jacket on the coat tree and put his on the hook next to it. Cozy.

He turned to find her standing in the entryway, gazing at him. The light was too dim to read her expression, but...the air between them seemed to crackle, and it wasn't because of the fire.

Did she want to follow up on that kiss? Or was she beginning to question this setup?

He'd rather not test what was creating the tension between them. "I didn't put the beer out since it would get warm. You could decide on which books while I fetch it." And get his bearings.

"Sounds great." She wandered over to the Dick Francis section of his bookcase.

"Want chips? Peanuts?" *Me*?

"No, thanks. Just a beer is fine."

"Be right back." He walked into the kitchen and automatically flipped on the light. Turned it off again.

"You okay in there?"

"Yep. Old habits die hard."

"You'll probably be glad when your corneas finally heal."

"I will." He opened the fridge and grabbed two bottles of McGavin's Pale Ale. "I have a pitcher of water, too," he called out. "Want some?"

"Maybe later."

He glanced toward the kitchen doorway where she stood backlit by the light from the living room.

"The wedding will be more brightly lit than this house."

"I know. Did you pick out some books?"

"I took four. Anyway, the wedding won't have spotlights glaring in your eyes or anything like that. Virginia's using a lot of battery-operated candles, but she wants the guests to be able to see what's going on. She also wants enough light for me to take some decent pictures."

"I understand."

She walked into the darkened kitchen. "You may not want to do this, but I think you should wear your shades."

Sweet of her to be concerned, but it was never going to be an issue. By Saturday night, Raven would no longer exist as a separate entity. His persona would be melded with Aaron's, who didn't need that level of eye protection. He prayed that she would forgive him this deception.

"Good suggestion." He twisted off a beer cap and handed her a bottle. "I'll keep it in mind."

She took the beer but made no move to leave the kitchen. "On the one hand, I'm glad you made it back in time for Badger's wedding. On the other, I worry that it'll be too hard on you."

"I'll manage."

"That's what concerns me." She moved closer and set her beer on the counter. "You'll suffer through whatever you need to so you can support Badger. He wouldn't want that and neither do I."

White-hot guilt stabbed him. He had no business misleading this compassionate woman, no matter what his motives were. Time to end the charade and be truthful. "I'm not—"

"You're not worried about yourself. I know! That's the problem! I like you, Raven. I like you a whole lot. I think you must like me a little bit, too."

"Of course…" He coughed. "Of course I do." How was he supposed to be noble when she was saying exactly what he wanted to hear?

"A little while ago, I kissed you."

"I noticed."

"If you wouldn't mind, I'd like to do it again."

His voice grew thick of its own accord. "I wouldn't mind."

"It's pretty dark in here. Think you could take off your cap?"

He sent it sailing toward the counter. Truth could wait. "First kiss was yours," he murmured. "This one's mine."

<u>6</u>

Caitlin's breath caught. This was the Raven she'd longed to meet, the bold warrior lurking just beneath the surface, the one she'd captured moments ago in her viewfinder. He drew her close without hesitation, circled her waist with one hand and cupped her cheek with the other.

His manner was so different that he could have been someone else, except when his velvet lips touched down. *Oh, yeah, it's you, Raven. Settle in. Stay awhile.*

Taste of mint. Clean scent of freshly shaven skin. Goodbye, bristle. He could freely demonstrate his talents, fully deploy his sensual mouth as he…yes, oh, yes…mmm…good….

He pulled her closer. Heat slid through her veins and settled between her thighs. She cupped the back of his head in both hands, pushed her fingers into his thick hair and slackened her jaw.

With a groan of pleasure, he tucked her into the curve of his aroused body. The firm thrust of his tongue released a quiver of flaming arrows aimed directly at her core. Fire licked her there, teasing, taunting.

He shifted the angle, intensified the connection. The coil of desire at her center tightened, wringing a whimper from her throat.

Pressing against his muscled body, she fit her hips to his and moaned in frustration. Her pulse raced when he pushed forward, telling her exactly what he wanted. What she wanted…

Gasping, he lifted his mouth from hers. "Wow."

She gulped for air. "Crazy."

"Yeah." He peppered her face with breathless kisses. "Fun, though."

"I never imagined—"

"We'd take off so fast?" He nibbled on her lower lip.

"No! Holy moly, Raven." She dragged in a shaky breath. "You'd better turn me loose."

"Don't want to."

"I don't want you to, but I know what…what this leads to."

"Good stuff."

She grasped for a lifeline of sanity in the whirlwind. "I'm…we're…not ready."

"Wanna bet?" He nuzzled behind her ear.

"M-mentally."

His chest heaved. "Fair enough." He kissed his way back to her mouth. His breath was warm against her damp lips, his voice low and gentle. "Tell me what you want."

You, naked. "Let's…let's sit by the fire. And…talk."

"Sure thing." He released her slowly and cleared his throat. "Go ahead. I'll be along."

"Okay." She picked up her beer from the counter, turned around and walked on unsteady legs into the living room. Had the easy chairs always been that close together? Yes, of course. The configuration was the same. It hadn't mattered before whether he was within touching distance.

Moving her camera to the table, she settled into the cushioned depths of the chair with a sigh. She craved a man who'd been a stranger until yesterday.

Technically a stranger. He'd never fit that category. She'd been at ease with him from the beginning, maybe because of the letter he'd written and maybe because of the details Badger had added.

She pressed the cool bottle to her flushed cheeks. Was this what people meant when they talked about chemistry? She'd always discounted the concept as justification for falling into bed with someone you barely knew. Evidently it was real, for her at least. She couldn't speak for him.

"I brought chips." He came in carrying a big bowl mounded with them. His cap was firmly in place, the brim tugged low to shade his eyes.

She set her camera on the floor beside her chair to make room for the bowl. "Did you bring chips so our mouths have something else to do?"

His laughter had a husky tinge to it. "Yep." He set down the bowl and his beer. "Fire needs tending." Turning his back, he crouched in front of the hearth.

His broad shoulders strained the material of his plaid shirt as he rearranged logs. He started to add one from the holder, paused and put it back. "Embers are nice, too."

Glowing coals also created a more intimate atmosphere. Was he going for that? He shifted position to grab a wrought-iron poker, and the worn denim of his jeans cupped and defined his tight backside. The man had a swoon-worthy body. If he made love as well as he kissed....

Whew. She pulled at the front of her shirt to dispel a sudden wave of heat. Reaching for a handful of chips, she started eating. Noisy darn things.

He chuckled. "Glad I brought those?"

"Yes." *Wish you'd brought ice cubes I could toss inside my shirt.* "I like chips."

"Me, too." He stood and replaced the screen.

She took another handful. "These are the best kind for eating plain. I only like the ridged ones for dipping."

"Same here." He sat down, picked up his beer and took a hefty swallow.

She waited, in case he had something he wanted to say first. Instead he picked up several chips and popped one in his mouth. She grabbed more chips and a helping of courage. "Let's talk about that kiss."

"All right." He took another swig of his beer.

She gazed at him as she munched. "Have you ever had a first kiss like that?"

"Wasn't the first." He scooped up another handful.

"The first one doesn't really count."

"Does so." He chewed and swallowed. "Why'd you do it?"

Good question. "I guess I was testing the waters to find out if saying I was beautiful meant you were into me."

"Short test."

"Long enough. You gasped. Then you trembled. That told me that you might be interested in another kiss."

"Which I was."

She looked over at him. He was staring into the fire. Without the bristle, the strong lines of his jaw were more prominent. He had a small white scar on the side of his cheek, probably from childhood, and a slight dip in the slope of his nose. "Did you break your nose?"

He nodded. "Basic training. Tripped." His cheek dented in a brief smile. "Not sure how my nose fits into the discussion, though."

"It doesn't. I just…never mind. My point is you're very good at kissing. For all I know, you create spontaneous combustion no matter who you're with. And that's what I want to know. Were you as blown away as I was?"

"*Blown away* is pretty vague."

"All right. On a scale of one to ten, that kiss for me was…a twenty."

"I see." His cheek creased in an even wider smile.

"How about you?"

He rubbed his chin. "I'd say…thirty-eight-point-six."

"What?"

"But we could both get to fifty-one-point-seven if we tried. Maybe even fifty-three-point-nine." There was a slight tremor running through his words like he was ready to bust out laughing.

"You're not taking this seriously."

"Oh, but I am." He put down his beer and pushed himself out of his chair. "Now that we've crunched the numbers, it's clear I have some work to do."

"Your voice sounds…better."

"Beer helps." Striding over to the floor lamp in the corner, he switched it off.

Her heart thumped faster. "Look, I didn't mean to turn this discussion into some sort of—"

"I know." He crossed the room to the other corner.

She leaned around the chair just as he clicked off the light hanging over a small dining table and chairs. He'd also turned off the lamp beside the front door.

The embers glowing in the fireplace provided the only light in the room. If he hadn't been looking at his phone, he would have been invisible. He tapped the screen and adjusted the volume on a country song.

The light from the screen stayed on for a moment after he laid the phone on the dining table. His back to her, he took off his hat and set it beside the phone.

The phone's screen went dark and he turned, a shadowy form as he walked toward her, his hand outstretched. "Caitlin Dempsey, may I have this dance?"

7

Aaron held his breath. He'd picked a song he happened to love, Ed Sheeran's *Perfect*. If Caitlin didn't like it, if she thought this move was cheesy and stupid, if—

"Yes, you may."

Sweet, sweet words. Sweeter yet was the warmth of her hand when she slipped it into his. Helping her up, he led her to the open area behind the chairs. The need to hold her was so strong he trembled with eagerness.

Not a lot of body contact in a waltz, but he'd do this first dance right. He was wooing, not seducing. One firm hand at her waist, the other held palm to palm, he used every bit of the small floor space.

She matched him step for step. "You can waltz." She sounded surprised.

"So can you."

"Mom and Dad taught me and my brother when we were kids."

"My mother taught me." He whirled her around.

"She did a good job. Can you see where you're going? Because I can't."

"Can't see much. I'm depending on my instrument readings."

She laughed. "Your instruments must be working."

"So far, so good." That about covered it. He couldn't ask for a better outcome than this—a passionate kiss followed by an elegant dance in an intimate setting.

Ever since their kiss, he'd eased up on the rasp in his voice. What a relief if he could get away with dropping it completely. For now, the lyrics of a love song spoke for him. And to him. Caitlin was all he'd imagined and more.

"This is lovely, Raven."

"Glad you like it." He'd listened to this song dozens of times, never danced to it. After this, it would be imprinted with the sound of her breathing, the scent of her perfume. "How's the song treating you?"

"One of my favorites."

Another positive sign. "What are some others?" With any luck, they'd be danceable and he'd have them on his phone.

"*Breathe* by Faith Hill."

Got it. "Then that'll be next."

"It's not a waltz."

"No worries. We can two-step."

"Is dancing okay for your leg?"

"My leg never felt better." The rest of him was having a good time, too. The song ended and he swung her around for a dramatic finish that made her giggle. "Stay right here so I can find you again."

"Okay." She sounded a little breathless.

Did she expect him to pull her into his arms and kiss her? Well, he'd do the unexpected and play the song she'd requested, instead. He'd summon the spirit of Raven, just as Badger had advised.

His eyes had adjusted enough that he could locate his phone on the table. He tapped on the Faith Hill album, chose the song and started it.

"Love this one."

"So do I." He walked back and gathered her into his arms so they could begin the dance. Or he could pull her closer, kiss those full lips and dive headfirst into paradise.

She swallowed. "Are we going to dance?"

"Yes. Yes, we are." He tightened his grip and off they went. Lots more body contact involved. He was more than okay with that aspect.

"Did your mom teach you the two-step?"

"Ryker did." He twirled her under his arm. "Before I was hurt, obviously. He said it was a required skill in Eagles Nest."

"He's right. Everybody dances the two-step around here."

"Where'd you learn?"

"Kendra." She was breathing faster as she executed the more vigorous movements. "I need practice, though."

"You're doing great."

"If I spent more nights on the dance floor at the Guzzling Grizzly and less time cooped up in my studio with Photoshop, I'd—whoops!" Her feet tangled with his.

"Easy." He steadied her so they wouldn't both go down.

"Thanks. See, I need practice."

"Practice with me." He cradled her loosely in his arms as Faith Hill crooned about the pleasures of making love. Took all he had to keep his touch light and casual.

"Tempting offer."

"Meant it to be." He drew her in gradually.

"Should we keep going, then?"

"Maybe later."

"Okay." She slid her hands up his chest. "You sound more relaxed."

"I do?"

"Clearly your throat has loosened up." She nestled against him.

"Guess so." All that delicious body contact was heating him up, but he needed to stay sharp. If she mentioned that his voice sounded familiar, he should have a response ready. Yeah, right. Strategizing and snuggling with Caitlin were mutually exclusive activities.

"I'm no physical therapist, but I think your throat issues might be related to anxiety."

"Could be." And maybe, just maybe, he was in the clear. "Makes sense if drinking beer helps."

"And spending time with me. Evidently I have a calming effect on you."

Evidently his voice was a non-issue. "Some parts yes, some parts no." He tightened his grip and aligned his hips with hers. "As you can clearly tell."

"You turn me on, too." She wound her arms around his neck. "I can't decide what to do about that."

"Are you open to suggestions?"

"Ah, Raven. You're a war hero with physical and mental scars, a vulnerable man of mystery. Have you any idea how seductive that is?"

"No, but I'm all ears."

"I'm a sucker for military guys. I wasn't kidding about being humbled by what you do."

"*Humbled* wasn't quite the word I was looking for. Doesn't have much of a ring to it." He combed her hair back from her face and slid his hand behind her nape. "How about *excited*?"

Her breath hitched. "That works."

"Aroused?" He leaned down.

"Uh-huh."

"Inflamed?"

"I'm getting there."

"Maybe I can help." He lowered his mouth to hers, going slow even though his body sizzled and burned, even though he could barely breathe, even though his jeans had become a torture device gripping his aching package.

He touched down lightly. Running the tip of his tongue over the velvet surface, he tasted salt. "Better than chips."

"Way better."

He settled in, caressing her mouth with gentle pressure as it softened beneath his. Then she sighed, parted those full lips and leaned into him. Any lingering resistance melted away.

Ah, Caitlin. Her mind might still be undecided, but her body had chosen. Her surrender washed over him like lava, obliterating restraint as he plunged his tongue into her hot mouth.

She groaned in response and gripped the back of his head. Giving as good as she got, she kissed him with wild abandon, digging her fingers into his scalp, wrapping one leg around his. When she started sucking on his tongue, he almost came.

He couldn't get enough of her mouth. Whenever she let loose of his tongue, he'd drive it deep as she whimpered and urged him on. Gripping her bottom, he picked her up. She straddled him, wound her legs around his hips and wiggled closer as she continued to make love to his tongue.

Carrying her to the table, he scooted her onto it. His cell phone went flying, hit the floor. When he urged her down to the table's surface, she bumped into something and knocked it over. A stack of books.

Didn't matter. All that mattered was Caitlin's irresistible mouth. He'd—

"Raven, stop." Her voice was breathy as she pushed against his chest.

"Why?"

"I just…I just knocked over Aaron's books."

"I don't—" By some miracle he swallowed the next word. And the swear words that would have followed it. He took a shaky breath. "The…ones…you're borrowing?"

"Yes." She took a breath. "I put them on the table."

"Didn't see 'em." He stepped back.

"I think one went on the floor."

"Oh."

"Where's your cap?"

"Left it next to my phone."

"Your phone?" She climbed off the table. "Is that what hit the floor first?"

"Yes."

"Then don't move." She dropped to her hands and knees. "Let me look for it. If you start walking around, you could step on it. It might already have a broken screen, but that can be repaired."

"I don't care about the phone."

"Well, I do. Your hat's probably down here, too. If I find it, we can turn on a light."

"Okay." Aaron's roommate Raven would be at least as concerned about the books as she was. Even if he was half-crazed from an interruption of what had promised to be—

What? Would he have taken her to bed? As she'd implied earlier, a make-out session that hot between two unattached, consenting adults usually had a logical conclusion. Would he have gone that route?

"Here's your phone." She handed it up to him. "Can you tell if the screen's cracked?"

He turned it toward the pale light from the fireplace. "Doesn't look like it."

"Good. I haven't found your—oh, wait, here it is." She gave him his hat.

"Thanks."

She stood. "Only one of Aaron's books fell. Keep your fingers crossed it isn't messed up. I won't be able to tell until you turn on the light."

"I know you're concerned, but Aaron's not that anal about his books."

"Whether he is or not, I don't want to be responsible for damaging them."

"You're not. I carried you over to the table." He put on his cap and tugged on the brim. Back to hiding, damn it.

"You didn't know the books were there. I did, but I forgot."

"They're probably fine." The lamp over the table was on a dimmer switch. He barely turned it on. "Is that enough?"

"Yes." She examined the book in her hands.

Nerve, one of his favorites. "Looks fine to me." He pulled the brim of his cap even lower so there was no chance she could see his eyes.

"Part of the dust jacket is bent."

"I'll bet it was like that."

"I'm not sure. I didn't examine each book. I just pulled out four I wanted. This was on top of the stack so that's why it fell."

"I'd be amazed if he'd get upset about a little dent. Probably came like that. He bought them used."

"From rare book dealers, from the looks of them."

"Not always." He wanted to kiss her again, hold her and convince her the condition of the dust jacket wasn't important. Couldn't kiss her with the hat on. Couldn't say that he didn't give a damn about a little dent.

She glanced at him. "You and Aaron have talked about the books?"

"Sure."

"That only proves my point that he cares about them."

"I guarantee he cares about people more."

"Of course he does. But still..." She sighed. "I wish I'd remembered I'd left them on the table."

"Regrets?"

"I regret that I knocked one of his books off the table." Her lips twitched as if she might be holding back a grin. "I don't regret what I was doing at the time."

"That's a relief."

"But I think I'd better head home." She glanced at him. "If I hadn't knocked over the books...would we have ended up in your bedroom?"

"Quite possibly." And if they had, would she have somehow discovered there was only one bed in this house?

"I think we would have, too." She straightened her blouse and ran her fingers through her hair. "In the heat of the moment."

"But not in the cool of the moment?"

"We just met yesterday, Raven."

"True, but—"

"Although I feel as if I've known you much longer."

"Same here." He was flying too close to the ground with that kind of talk. If he didn't pull up, he might crash. He needed to land safely and regroup. "I'll get your jacket."

"Thanks. I'll grab my camera." After gathering up the books, she fetched her camera from the floor beside her chair and walked toward him. "I'll probably tell Aaron I accidentally dropped one of these."

He took the books and camera so she could put on her jacket. "Not going to mention we were making out on the table?"

"Probably not."

"Will I see you tomorrow night?"

"Do you want to?"

"Silly question."

"Then I'll be here."

He couldn't hold back a smile. "Great."

"What about Aaron?"

"What about him?"

"I figure eventually he'll be home when I come to visit you."

"Oh. Not tomorrow night, though. He's got another run to Casper."

"I'll bet he volunteers for all these night flights so Ryker and Badger can stay home with their sweetie-pies."

"Hadn't thought of that."

"I wouldn't be surprised. That sounds like him."

"It does, at that. Considerate guy."

"Very." She leaned over, ducked under his cap and gave him a quick peck on the mouth. "So are you."

"Thank you."

She opened the door. "And for your information, on a scale of one to ten, I rate that kiss an eighty-seven-point-nine." She flashed him a smile and stepped onto the very dark porch. He quickly flicked on the porch light and closed the door.

He forgave himself for not remembering to turn on the light for her. He'd just participated in the kiss of the century. She'd ranked it, but he couldn't assign a number to that episode. It was off the charts.

_8_

The next morning Caitlin overslept after staying up late trying various editing effects on her pictures of Raven. For her favorite of the bunch, she'd chosen a sepia tone to give the scene a World War II look.

She wouldn't mind having it as her screensaver. Framed by the sunset, hands shoved in the pockets of his flight jacket and aviators adding mystery to his expression, he embodied her fantasy of a war hero returning home to his loved ones.

She'd show it to him tonight on her laptop, but if he still wanted all the shots deleted, she'd have to stick by her promise. She loved them, though, especially that one, so maybe she'd be able to convince him they were worth keeping.

Oversleeping meant she rushed through breakfast and took the quickest shower in history. Damp hair braided and lipstick on, she drove to Virginia's wedding venue for an eight o'clock appointment.

The meeting to discuss lighting for the ceremony was likely unnecessary. Caitlin had shot several weddings there and knew what worked, but Virginia was micromanaging every aspect of this one. Understandable given that she was the mom of two of the participants.

She pulled into the parking lot with two minutes to spare. Virginia's SUV was there and so was Badger's red truck. Interesting. She'd planned to call him today to give him an update. If he'd come without Hayley, maybe she could accomplish that after the meeting.

Schematics in a zipped portfolio, she walked into the renovated barn that had become a popular wedding chapel. Virginia had preserved the rustic atmosphere, but the building was now insulated and temperature-controlled. The venue had a top-of-the-line sound system and antique light fixtures controlled from a hidden panel could create various effects.

Evidently Virginia had recruited Badger to help her test the lights. He stood in front of the open panel adjusting dials while she roamed the venue calling out instructions. As tall as Hayley, she was still blond thanks to the hairdressers at Shear Delight. She could be mistaken for her daughter, especially from a distance, but Caitlin had spent enough time with them to spot the differences.

Virginia glanced toward the back of the chapel. "Ah, Caitlin! Perfect! You can tell us the optimal setting that will work with the lights you're bringing."

"Whatever you've done before has been fine. Hi, Badger."

"Hi, Caitlin." He tipped his hat and smiled.

"Fine isn't good enough," Virginia said. "I'm going for subtle and atmospheric, but it's tricky. A subtle effect can turn lackluster."

"I can guaran-damn-tee this weddin' won't be lackluster." Badger closed the panel and walked down the aisle toward Caitlin. "Agreed?"

"Absolutely. It'll have luster coming out of its ears."

"I know, right? We're stuffin' the whole place with flowers, Bryce and Nicole are providin' the music and the weddin' party is a handsome bunch. As if that's not enough to push everyone's happy button, there'll be me, rockin' out on the bagpipes. How could it be lackluster with all that goin' on?"

She grinned. "I can't imagine."

"You need to let me hear you play those pipes," Virginia said. "Makes me nervous that I have no idea what you'll sound like."

"I'll sound like a Highlander standin' on the moor serenadin' his lady."

"I still want to hear you do it before the ceremony so I—"

"Virginia, darlin'." He walked over and put his arm around her shoulders. "You know I love you to pieces."

"That's neither here nor there." A smile tugged at the corners of her mouth.

"If I had in mind to let anyone hear me play besides Aleck, that person would be you."

"Then why not—"

"Because my playin' will exceed your expectations, and Hayley will find out you heard me play and pester you for details."

"I won't give her any details."

"You won't need to. She'll see the gleam in your eye and *her* expectations will go up. So far her expectations are like yours, on the low side, which is just where I want 'em. I'm fixin' to blow her away."

Caitlin pressed her lips together to keep from laughing. Badger relished this kind of drama, and he had a talent for it. Fortunately, he only used his powers for good.

"Oh, all right." Virginia's smile broke through. "You win. I won't pester you any more about it."

"Thank you, ma'am. I truly appreciate your understandin'."

"Yeah, yeah. You know I'm a sucker for your wiles, Badger. Now if you'll please step over to the control panel and show Caitlin the full range of the lighting options, we can figure out how to coordinate our efforts."

"Yes, ma'am."

"I came in while you were testing," Caitlin said. "Didn't I just see your lighting options?"

"That's the original set and I wanted to make sure we don't have any crossed wires." Virginia joined her in the aisle between the rows of pew-style wooden seats. "A company just finished installing additional lights." She pointed to the ceiling. "They did a great job of making them unobtrusive."

"Sure did." Caitlin glanced up. "Tiny dudes."

"Very high tech. Now we can add washes of color to the regular lighting. That's one reason I didn't schedule any weddings in here this week, so I could have this done."

"I can't wait to show it off," Badger said. "Lightin' is the soul of any event."

Virginia leaned closer. "And he paid for it," she murmured.

"Wow." But then, Badger was known for his generosity. Rumor had it that he'd managed his trust fund well and clearly he enjoyed spreading the wealth.

With Virginia directing the action, Badger demonstrated the new system's capabilities. It could bathe the rustic walls in a single color, such as gold, or alternate complimentary shades. The technology could be fun to work with but she'd need to set up her umbrella lights and do a trial run before Saturday.

When Badger had gone through all the combinations, Virginia turned to her. "Cool, huh?"

"Very cool. The guests will love it."

"Can you work with it?"

"Sure. But I'll need to take some practice shots before Saturday and I didn't bring any of my equipment this morning."

"I could probably arrange to be here tonight or tomorrow night, if you'd like to come back then."

She hated to cancel one of her nights with Raven. Maybe she wouldn't have to. "How about if I come over on Friday afternoon, instead?"

"I couldn't make it then. I'll be in the thick of things with the rehearsal and rehearsal dinner, and—"

"I'll do it on Friday afternoon." Badger joined them.

"You can't," Virginia said. "You're in the wedding party. I'm sure Hayley—"

"I'll check with her, but I'm bettin' she won't mind if I come over here early to handle this. She knows I'm all about the lightin' effects."

"You're probably right. She's thrilled that you're so involved in the wedding preparations, more so than she is."

"Because I'm Southern. We're all about the weddin'."

Virginia patted his cheek. "I do think you and I are the most dedicated to making this event shine."

"That puts me in good company."

"Thank you, sweet boy." She gave him a kiss on the cheek. "I hate to shoo you both out of here, but I'm meeting the Whine and Cheese Club for coffee at Pie in the Sky in fifteen minutes. They've asked me to be a member."

"Aw." Caitlin smiled. "That's wonderful."

"Sure is," Badger said. "I hadn't heard about that."

"I'm excited. They haven't added a new member since Jo Fielding was invited, and that was years ago."

Badger gave her a hug. "They made a great choice in addin' you." Then he gestured toward the door. "After you, ladies."

Once they were outside, Virginia bid them a quick goodbye, hopped in her SUV and drove out of the parking lot.

Badger gazed after her. "She'll love bein' in the Whine and Cheese Club."

"She will. I'm so glad they asked her." On a hunch, she glanced up at him. "Did you have anything to do with it?"

He shrugged. "Not much, really. Kendra said they'd already been considerin' it."

"And you lobbied in her favor."

"The timin' is right. Marryin' off her kids has been her focus for years. Sometimes I see wistfulness in her eyes, like *what now?* Those ladies will help her figure that out."

"You're a good man, Badger Calhoun."

He grinned. "Don't let that get around, darlin'. It's more fun if folks think I'm a scalawag."

"Good luck with pulling that off. Listen, did you just happen to be here or did you arrange it so you'd be—"

"Took advantage of a golden opportunity. Figured you and I might have a chance to talk about our joint project."

"Thought so." She smiled. "And thanks for volunteering to help me on Friday afternoon. I didn't want to give up one of my nights with Raven."

"That's good news."

"He's a great guy. I'm glad you brought us together."

"See, I knew you two would hit it off."

"We definitely do, and your little *experiment* is working like a charm."

"The experiment. Right."

"If you were concerned that he couldn't deal with the wedding, you can quit worrying. But I advised him to wear his shades."

"Ah. That's a thought."

"He's made so much progress, though. The first night he was unshaven, like he was in hiding, so to speak. But last night he'd shaved."

"Really?"

"I think it's a sign of progress. He looks so much better that way, so much happier."

"I'll just bet he does."

"And that's not all. Have you talked to him lately?"

"No, as a matter of fact, but I plan to."

"You'll be amazed by his voice. I think spending time with me has helped his vocal cords relax. He sounds almost normal, now."

"Wow, that's truly amazin'. Thanks for lettin' me know. I can't wait to have a conversation with that boy."

"I think you'll be pleased."

"I wasn't expectin' such fast...progress. Is he still wearin' that ball cap he's so attached to?"

"He is, except when we're...dancing." Why couldn't she have just said *yes*? Now Badger was staring at her as if she was demented.

"Where would you be doin' that?"

"In the living room."

"With the lights on?"

"He turned them off."

"Ah. What about music? Did he hire a band to play tunes on the front porch?"

She laughed. "You're funny. He used the music on his phone."

"Okay, but that livin' room is no bigger than a minute, so I can't picture how—"

"We managed. He's a very good dancer. I guess you already know that if you were on hand when Ryker was teaching him the two-step."

"He mentioned that, did he?"

"He's mentioning all kinds of things as he starts to open up. I can see why you and Aaron like him so much." Time for a change of subject. "Speaking of Aaron, am I right that he volunteers for all the night flights because he's single and you and Ryker aren't?"

"Why, uh...*yes, ma'am*! You nailed it! That's exactly the situation. That's Aaron, all right. Considerate as they come."

"It's touching that he'd do that. Even though I haven't spent much time with him, I feel like I know him a little better because I've been in his house. Last night I borrowed some of his Dick Francis books."

"You're a fan?"

"Huge fan."

"So is Aaron! What a coincidence. I can picture you two havin' a big ol' time talkin' 'bout Dick Francis books."

"I would love that, except yesterday Ryker confirmed my suspicion that Aaron has a crush on me, so I—"

"You talked to Ryker?"

"Don't worry. Raven warned me not to say anything about him being in town. Personally, I think Ryker would want to know, but that's not my call."

"We'll tell him on Friday."

"Good, because whatever experiment you and Raven are doing, I feel sure Ryker would understand and be supportive."

"Possibly. Anyway, thanks for not mentionin' it yesterday. What did Ryker say, exactly?"

"That Aaron admired me. Then he asked if I could possibly get past the name problem."

"Do you think you could?"

"I doubt it. But that's not the only reason I won't go out with him. Now I have another one."

"Which is?"

"I've developed feelings for Raven."

Badger coughed. "I see." He cleared his throat. "Well, that's not all bad."

"I don't think it's bad at all. Maybe a little awkward, since he and Aaron are roommates, but I think Aaron would be understanding."

"You know what? I guarantee he would."

9

Aaron was drinking a last cup of coffee before heading to the airfield when Badger's red truck pulled up outside. Coffee mug in hand, he walked over and opened the door as Badger came striding up the walk, a determined set to his jaw.

"Hey, Badger. I've got about ten minutes. Want coffee?"

"No, thanks, Romeo. Just need a moment of your time."

"I'm guessing you talked to Caitlin." He stepped back from the door.

"Just now." Badger walked into the living room, nudged back his Stetson and stared at him without speaking.

"What?"

"Are you *tryin'* to blow this carefully calibrated scheme to smithereens?"

"Could be." He hadn't unpacked his mental suitcase yet. No telling what motivations he'd find in there.

"Well, you're doin' a damn good job of it. The good news is she's crazy about you."

His breath caught. "She said that?"

"Not her exact words. She said she's *developed feelings* for you. But if you'd seen the look in her eyes, you'd—"

"Damn." He scrubbed a hand over his face.

"I thought you'd be happy."

"I am. And confused. Mostly I think I'm screwed."

"I could've told you that. Shouldn't have shaved off the bristle, hot shot. Now you can't show your face in town for the next two days."

"That's the least of my problems."

"Bit off more'n you could chew?"

"You could say that." He grimaced. "I almost took her to bed last night."

Badger's jaw dropped. "*No.*"

"Yep."

"Well, dill my pickle."

"Yeah. I'm an idiot."

"May I remind you that the stagin' area for the mission is *here*?" He swept a hand around the living room. "Raven's fictional world ends at the entrance to the hallway. Beyond that lies Aaron Donahue Land. Step across that line and the magic is over."

"Sort of lost track of that last night."

"You'd better sort of keep track of it tonight. Unless you're plannin' to furnish that second bedroom in the next few hours."

"I'm ashamed to admit this, but I checked on renting a bedroom set."

"Please tell me you came to your senses."

"I could have one delivered late this afternoon after I'm back from Kalispell, which would give me just enough time to rearrange the second bedroom before she gets here."

"Oh, Lordy."

"I didn't order it."

Badger exhaled. "I'm relieved as a forgiven sinner, but how come you didn't?"

"Finally realized it was a good thing she knocked the books off the table."

Badger's eyes widened. "You were makin' whoopee on the table?"

"Yeah, but that's not important. The point is—"

"Damn, good buddy. I severely underestimated your sex appeal."

"Raven's sex appeal. And that's the point. I'd be making love to her as Raven, not me."

"But Raven *is* you."

"Only part of me.

"The part that gets the action, evidently. Never occurred to me you'd be canoodlin' on a tabletop by Day Two."

He sighed. "She probably thinks tonight's the night."

"Shavin' was your first mistake. Tried to talk you out of it. If you'd listened to ol' Badger, you wouldn't be standin' here wonderin' how to stop this runaway train."

"Can't be standing here thinking about it any longer, either. I'm wheels up in thirty. Don't you have a run today, too?"

"As a matter of fact, I'm fetchin' a couple of weddin' guests from Missoula. I need to get goin'."

"Then we're outta here." He grabbed his flight jacket, his Stetson and his keys before following Badger out the door. "I'd appreciate any suggestions you might have for cooling things down tonight."

Badger chuckled. "You do realize this is a horse and barn door situation."

"Yeah, but I'm desperate. I'll consider whatever your fertile brain can supply."

"How 'bout comin' down with a highly contagious disease?"

"Other than that. Gross."

"Answer's obvious, then. Let your bristle grow."

* * *

Because he couldn't come up with a better idea, Aaron resigned himself to not shaving before Caitlin arrived. His bristle could scour the rust off a tailpipe. He wouldn't be tempted to kiss her with the equivalent of steel wool on his face. Scruff as chastity belt.

But while he was laying the fire, he changed his mind. Damn it, he hated that look on himself. Besides, she'd interpret the scruff as a psychological step backward. She'd be disappointed and that didn't sit well with him.

He'd almost run out of time to correct the situation, though. Leaving the fire unlit, he raced back to his bathroom, tossed his cap on the counter, stripped off his shirt and lathered up. A fast shave was better than no shave.

Or not. He nicked himself. Stemming the bleeding with a piece of TP, he finished just as she rang the doorbell.

"Be right there!" He shoved his arms into the sleeves of his shirt and fumbled with the buttons. To hell with it. He'd rather answer the door with his shirt unbuttoned than with TP stuck to his face.

He carefully peeled it away. The bleeding had stopped. Blotting his damp cheeks with the towel, he hung it around his neck before heading into the living room. *His cap.*

He ran back for it, crammed it on his head and bolted for the door. He was panting by the time he opened it. "Hi."

"Hi." Her warm gaze traveled over him. "I'm a little early. Didn't mean to rush you."

"Poor time management on my part." He stepped back to let her in. "I was laying the fire when I remembered I hadn't shaved."

"Since yesterday?"

"Since this morning." He tried to regulate his breathing, but seeing her again made that a challenge.

"Your beard grows that fast?"

"Yep." He started buttoning his shirt. "I see you brought your laptop."

"I did."

He stopped buttoning and held out his hand. "Let me take—"

"You cut yourself." She tucked the laptop securely under her arm, stepped closer and cupped his chin with her free hand. Her fingers whispered like butterfly wings over his damp skin.

His heart thundered as he zeroed in on her beautiful mouth. "Amateur mistake. I was hoping you wouldn't notice." He was seconds away from kissing her. Did he have a plan for avoiding that? No.

"I'm touched that you rushed to get a shave in before I got here." She stroked her thumb along his jawline. "I had no idea shaving was a twice-a-day chore for you."

"'Fraid so." Her sweet mouth beckoned. If he didn't manufacture a distraction ASAP, he would pull her into his arms, computer and all.

Once he did that, he'd likely lose his mind as he had the night before. He'd ignore Badger's mission boundaries, break through the invisible barrier in the hall and plunge into Aaron Donahue Land because a bed was there.

Think, Donahue. You're smarter than this. He took a quick breath. "You know what we should do?"

"I have a few ideas." Her blue eyes had gone all smoky. "Tell me yours and I'll tell you mine."

"Since I haven't lit the fire yet, we could go for a drive."

She frowned in confusion. "Why?"

"It's a beautiful night and I feel the need to escape these four walls."

Her expression cleared. "Of course you do. I didn't stop to think you might be going stir-crazy. Evening would be the perfect time for you to get some fresh air. I totally understand. We can take my Cherokee."

"Or we could take my truck."

"That's your truck parked in the driveway? I thought it was Aaron's."

"It's mine."

"Now that you say that, I don't know why I thought it was Aaron's. His is at the airport, isn't it?"

"Mm." He walked the thin line between truth and fiction.

"Okay, then. I'll just leave my laptop here for later." She set it on the table.

He couldn't spend any time looking at that table or he'd want to replay last night's tape. But first he'd move her laptop. He finished buttoning his shirt. "Why'd you bring it?"

"You know those pictures I took of you yesterday while we were outside?"

"Oh, right. We never did look at them." Otherwise occupied.

"I finally did check them out after I got home. I really like them. I fooled around with a few special effects and I wanted to show you how they look."

"That'd be great." He was amazed that even after studying all those images, she didn't have a clue about his identity. Badger had counted on her eagerness to believe Raven's story and evidently he'd been on the money.

Pocketing his keys, he put on his flight jacket before opening the door. A soft twilight and a clear sky greeted him. He took a deep breath of cool air. Dodged a bullet, at least for now.

"I'm glad you suggested this." Caitlin glanced back at him before starting down the steps. "It is a beautiful night. I've been so busy rushing from one thing to another that I haven't paused to appreciate how gorgeous the September weather is right now."

"I'm sure you have your hands full between senior pictures and a big wedding." He walked around to the passenger side and opened her door. The dome light came on. "Whoops, bright light."

She hopped in and reached for the switch. "Got it. How'd you know about the senior pictures?"

How, indeed? "Aaron mentioned it."

"He must have talked with Kendra about my sessions out at Wild Creek."

"He did." And it had sparked an idea. Closing her door, he rounded the front of the truck and climbed behind the wheel. "I guess there are times Kendra can't accommodate the kids." He closed his door and buckled his seat belt.

"Well, sure. I work around that as best I can."

"Would it help to have an alternate venue for those times?" He started the truck and backed out of the drive.

"Yes, and Kendra even suggested I look at other ranches in the area. I did, but none of them have the fantastic photographic possibilities that Wild Creek offers. The kids would assume they were getting second tier, and they'd be right."

"Not another ranch. Badger Air."

"Badger Air? You mean the planes and stuff?"

"Exactly. I think—" He coughed. "Aaron thinks it's a natural. Graduating seniors are taking flight into the next phase of their lives, so what better way to illustrate it than posing them in and around planes?"

"It's an excellent idea. Has Aaron said anything to Badger or Ryker?"

"Not yet. He might have wanted to ask if you'd be interested before he talked with them."

"Most definitely. I'll bet some of those seniors would love posing with a plane."

"I sure would've at their age."

"You're excited about this idea, aren't you?"

"I am."

"You're hoping to get a job with Badger Air, right?"

"Yes, ma'am."

"I can see you having fun working with those teenagers. If Ryker and Badger go for the concept, maybe you could be the liaison for the photography project."

"I'd like that."

"So would I." No mistaking the undercurrent running through her words. "Where are we going, by the way?"

"Oh, just out in the country, away from the lights of town so we can see some stars." Far from Aaron Donahue Land and the box of condoms in his bedside table drawer.

Maybe he was splitting hairs. If he was, so be it. Making out in the boonies carried a lot less weight than renting furniture and inviting her into his bed. That was his story and he was sticking to it.

"Raven, are we going out parking?" She sounded amused.

"I guess you could call it that. Do you think it's a lame idea?"

"I think it's sweet and romantic." She reached over and squeezed his thigh. "Like you." She left her hand where it was.

The warmth from her hand spread over his thigh and traveled inevitably to his family jewels. From the frying pan into the fire....

_10_

What a fascinating man, this Raven. When he'd come to the door freshly shaven with his shirt hanging open, Caitlin had almost swallowed her tongue. Muscular pecs decorated with a sprinkling of jet-black chest hair? Yes, please.

She'd longed to get her hands on all that masculine yumminess ASAP. The unlit fire had been a clear signal that he was ready to light hers.

Pheromones had swirled. She'd stroked his jaw and he'd sucked in a breath. They'd seemed to be on the same page, ready for that walk down the hall in search of Nirvana.

Then he'd suggested this drive, clearly plucking the idea out of thin air. Whatever the plan had been, he wasn't following it anymore. Ravens were inventive. He'd told her so the first night and demonstrated it the second night with his unexpected invitation to dance.

On night three, instead of taking her to bed, he was behind the wheel of his truck, spiriting her away to a night of stargazing and hot kisses. She couldn't wait to find out what happened on night four.

Sitting in the passenger seat gave her a new perspective, though. In the easy chairs, she'd studied his profile from the left. She had the right-side view tonight.

The light from the dash revealed a small mole on his right cheekbone, not far from his hairline. A tiny dot of dried blood marked the spot where he'd nicked himself. No doubt he'd rushed to shave so he could kiss her with those sculpted lips.

While messing with the photos of him, she'd enlarged the image, traced the outline of his mouth and relived his wild, passionate kisses. Surely he wouldn't insist that she get rid of the pictures.

"Mighty quiet over there."

"I was thinking about the shots I took of you yesterday. You were a reluctant subject."

"Uh-huh."

"Have you always been camera-shy or is that a more recent thing?"

"More recent."

"Well, thank you for indulging me, then. I'm hoping I can talk you into letting me keep those shots. I wouldn't do anything with them without your permission."

"I know you wouldn't. You can hang onto them. It's okay."

"Yay! Thank you. I think you'll like what I've done with one of the shots. It suits you."

His cheek creased in a smile. "Now I'm curious."

"Good. That's my goal." She gazed at his profile. That darned cap did an excellent job of throwing the top third of his face in dark shadow. "What color are your eyes?"

"Brown."

"Light brown or dark brown?"

"Light, I guess. My mom says they're almost golden."

"I understand that you need to protect them, but I look forward to a time you're healed enough that you don't have to wear either the cap or the shades. It'll be a big day when I can look in your eyes."

His chest heaved. "Yes, it will." He put on the left turn signal and slowed the truck. Ever since leaving the outskirts of town, traffic had been almost nonexistent.

"You seem to know where you're going."

"I do." He swung the truck onto the dirt road and the rough surface crunched under the tires. "You might have missed the sign a ways back."

"Guess so." She'd been too busy looking at him.

"About a half-mile down this road is a trailhead. There's a pretty little meadow at the base of the trail."

"How did you know about it?"

"Aaron's a hiker." He slowed the truck to a crawl. "He found it."

"I didn't know he liked to hike."

"Yeah, he gets teased about that a lot."

"I'm sure. Cowboys prefer to ride."

"But he does both, so some of the guys give him a hard time about not being a true cowboy."

"To heck with them. If he likes both, he should do both."

"That's what I say. When—" He stepped on the brakes. "Fox just ran across. Did you see it?"

"I did! A night hike would be fun, wouldn't it?"

"Yeah. Wearing my boots tonight, though."

"Me, too. I didn't mean now. Do you hike?"

"I do."

"On cloudy days, probably."

"Cloudy days are nice. And the exercise is great for my leg."

"Do you ride, too?"

"I love to ride."

"When you're ready to reveal that you're here, you need to go out to Wild Creek Ranch and ride there. Aaron's probably already told you that, but I'll add my vote. Kendra has the best horses and the prettiest trails in this area."

"Sounds great."

"I'd go with you, if you want company."

"Absolutely." He pulled into a clearing and drove around it so the nose of the truck faced the road. "We're here." He shut off the engine and turned off the headlights.

"Now that's what I call dark."

"The moon's not up over the mountains, yet. Do you have your phone?"

"In my pocket. How about you?"

"Yep. We'd better use the flashlight so we don't trip. That's assuming you want to get out."

"Of course I do. How else will we see the stars?"

He chuckled. "Right." The click of his seat belt indicated he'd soon be on the move.

She'd already unbuckled. "Meet you by the tailgate."

"I'll be right there. I want to see if I can find something."

"Okay." She opened her door, turned on her flashlight app and hopped down.

Dry grass and fallen leaves crackled under her boots as she walked around to the back of the truck. She hadn't been parking with a guy for years and never with someone as interesting as Raven.

What was his last name? He must have one, but Badger hadn't mentioned it and neither had Raven when they'd met. Maybe it was dull and boring or long and unpronounceable. That would suck the cool right out of being called *Raven*. Better not to ask.

But what was he doing? Rummaging around for some reason. "I'm getting lonely back here," she called out.

"Sorry." He closed the driver's door. "Thought I had a blanket behind the seat. I don't. Should've planned better."

She laughed. "It was perfectly obvious you didn't plan this *at all*."

"That's a fact." He came toward her, his flashlight pointed at the ground. "Acted totally on impulse."

"It was a good impulse." Now that he was here with his flashlight, she switched hers off and tucked the phone in her pocket again.

"A blanket would have been nice, though. We're not gonna lie on the cold, hard ground."

"You could put down the tailgate. We could sit on that and…look at the stars."

"Is it possible you've done this a time or two?"

"Maybe."

"Then a tailgate party it is. Hold this for me, please." He handed her his phone.

She kept the light pointed toward the ground as he lowered the tailgate with a thump. She glanced at it. Kind of high off the ground. She might have to step on the back bumper to—

She squeaked as he grabbed her around the waist and swung her up. Didn't groan or gasp while executing that move, either. "Thanks!"

"You bet." He pulled himself up beside her. "I can take the phone back."

She handed it to him, making sure she directed the light away from his eyes. "You've been keeping in shape."

"I'd get frustrated about my leg not healing as fast as I wanted, so I'd work on my upper body."

"You do good work."

"Glad you approve." Turning the light away from him, he propped the phone against the wheel well creating a soft, ambient glow. "For atmosphere."

"Lovely."

"Well, here we are."

"Here we are." She glanced up. "And look at all those stars."

"Can I tell you a secret?"

"Sure. I love secrets."

"I don't give a damn about the stars right now."

She turned to him. Thanks to the glow from his phone, he'd become a vague outline, differentiated from the dark cluster of pine trees surrounding the clearing. "Are you saying that you dangled the prospect of stargazing so that you could get me alone and have your way with me?"

"Yes, ma'am."

"Then what are you waiting for?"

"I was hoping you'd climb into my lap and put some moves on me." Laughter rippled through his words.

"I can barely see you. I could miss your lap entirely and end up on the ground."

"Guess I'll have to help the process along, then. Maneuver you over here."

"Okay. Any stacks of books lying around?"

"Nope. Wait. Let's take off our jackets so our phones are safe."

"If I take off my jacket, I'll need someone to keep me warm."

"All part of the plan."

"I'm beginning to think you've done this a time or two, yourself." She shrugged out of her jacket, folded it and laid it nearby.

"Could be. First I need to get a good grip." He fumbled a bit before grasping her by the waist. "Gotcha."

"That was fun." Heat radiated out from the point of contact. She quivered in anticipation.

"Not my smoothest move, but things will improve from here on. When I pick you up, hold onto my shoulders and slide your legs around my hips."

She gripped his broad shoulders as he lifted her neatly onto his lap. "Your upper body strength is truly impressive."

"If I'd known I was in training for this, I would have worked twice as hard."

"Speaking of hard, I just came in contact with—"

"I'm aware of that." Bracketing her hips, he adjusted her position so she rested on his thighs instead of being tucked right up against his package. "Ah, that's better."

"Years ago I would never have mentioned it."

"Years ago I wouldn't have, either."

"Now I'm wondering, since you hustled me out of the house so fast, if you brought—"

"I didn't. Kinda on purpose."

"Trying to slow things down a bit?"

"I am." Sliding his hands up her back, he gently massaged her shoulders. "Do you mind?"

"I don't mind, but I'm surprised. Last night we almost ended up in your bedroom."

"Because my brain had totally checked out. I wasn't sure how tonight would go, but I was hoping I'd figure out a way to postpone that step a little longer."

She cupped his bristle-free face in both hands and smoothed her thumbs over his cheekbones. "Because it'll mean more if we do?"

"Exactly."

"You're an unusual guy, Raven."

"I'll take that as a compliment."

"Please do. I'm attracted to that quality. I like the idea that we're holding off. That said, I sure hope we'll have full-throttle, mind-blowing sex eventually."

"If I have anything to say about it, we will."

"You'll have plenty to say about it."

"Maybe. Maybe not." Cradling her head in one hand, he wrapped an arm around her shoulders and drew her closer. "But when that time comes, I hope you'll remember this." He dipped his head and laid claim to her mouth.

_11_

With a groan of pleasure, Aaron gave himself up to the joy of kissing Caitlin. Even if this crazy episode ended in disaster, he'd have a night under the stars when she wanted him as much as he wanted her.

She kissed him back with such energetic gusto that he lost his balance. Laughing, he broke their fall as best he could. Thank God the truck bed had a rubberized surface. Now they were horizontal, which was more convenient, anyway. "You okay?" He drew her close.

"I will be once you start kissing me again."

"Same here." In seconds, they were plastered together as if they were magnetized. He fumbled with her clothes and she reached for his shirt buttons. He got hers unfastened first.

"No fair." She grabbed handfuls of his partially open shirt. "Take this off before I rip it off."

He sat up, pulled it over his head and tossed it aside. By the time he turned back and reached to unfasten her bra, he touched only warm, silky Caitlin. No bra, no shirt.

"Mm, nice." He explored slowly, reverently, cupping and releasing the weight of each plump breast. "Wish I could see."

"Me, too. But I can finally touch." She splayed both hands over his chest. "Feels even better."

"Better than what?"

"Better than I imagined when you came out with your shirt hanging open. Remember that?"

"Well, yeah, but—"

"I almost attacked you." She pressed her fingers into his pecs. "When a guy with a chest like yours leaves his shirt open...let's just say it activates a hormonal response."

His breathing roughened. "I didn't have time to button it."

"Likely story. You were trying to get me hot."

"I wasn't, but if that's what works..." Leaning down, he feathered a kiss over her lips.

"Like a charm." She slid her arms around his neck. "Bring that hot body down here, big guy. I'm feeling a chill."

"Can't have that." Balanced on his forearms, he eased down until he lightly touched her soft breasts. Swaying from side to side, he created a sensual friction. "Warmer, now?"

Her breath caught. "Much warmer."

"Let's try this." Shifting his position, he cradled one breast in his palm and circled her taut nipple with his tongue. Then he raked the tight bud with his teeth.

She gasped and arched her back, silently begging for more...and more she would have. Kneading gently with his fingers, he drew her sensitive nipple into his mouth, rolling it over his tongue, sucking rhythmically, building the tension.

Her hips moved restlessly beneath him. Slowly but surely, she was coming undone. With him. Fierce joy swelled in his chest.

His groin throbbed, but he ignored it as he kissed a path to her other breast. Her labored breathing turning to panting desperation. *"Raven...please..."*

While continuing to caress her with his lips and tongue, he unfastened her jeans. She made a low, humming sound deep in her throat. He pulled the zipper down and slipped his hand under the elastic of her panties. She dragged in a breath.

His cock strained against the restriction of unforgiving denim. But he'd made his choice when he'd left the house. Not tonight. Ah, but she was ready. How sweet it would be to sink deep into.... Never mind.

He reached lower and slid his fingers through her damp curls. She was drenched. Pushing two fingers deep, he pressed his thumb against her trigger point.

Didn't take long. A few strokes and she came, gasping and crying out his name. *Raven.*

His jaw clenched. *Aaron.* He gulped in air. It was okay. Fine. If fortune smiled on him, if he was given the privilege of taking her to bed...Aaron Donahue would be the man loving her.

Would that ever happen? No telling. For now he'd hold her until her trembling stopped and she relaxed in his arms. Her skin was damp, so he'd cover her with his body so she wouldn't get chilled. He had enough heat coursing through his veins to keep her warm all night long.

Taking a deep breath, she let it out in a long, satisfied sigh. "That was so wonderful."

"I'm glad."

"One-sided, though."

"Nope. I enjoyed every minute of making you happy."

She combed his hair back from his forehead. "Then how about letting me enjoy making *you* happy?"

"That's a tempting offer, but we're not going there."

"Why not?"

"I'm not sure I can answer that in a way that makes sense."

"Please try." She cupped his cheek. "It seems unfair that I'm lying here blissed out while you have a case of blue balls."

He laughed. "Boldly stated."

"I said that just to make you laugh. But since the subject is on the table, I always wondered. Do they literally turn blue?"

"Not that I could tell. I'll be fine."

"I could make you finer."

"I'm sure you could, but..."

"Are you shy about having a woman do that?"

"Hell, no."

She wiggled against him. "Then let me."

"No, thank you."

"I don't get it."

He cleared his throat. "I wrote that letter asking you to spend some time with me. The idea was that we'd have some nice conversations, get to know each other."

"Which we did."

"We did, and we sailed way beyond that."

"I'm thrilled about that! These evenings with you have been so special."

"For me, too."

"I mean, top priority. Virginia suggested I come over to the wedding venue either tonight or tomorrow night to test my equipment with the new lights she's had installed. I wasn't willing to cancel with you so I told her I had another commitment both nights."

"I'm honored, but don't you need to do that before the wedding?"

"I will. I told her I could test the lights on Friday afternoon before the rehearsal. She can't be there at that time because she'll be wrangling out-of-town guests and such, but Badger offered to come early and help me. He probably didn't want me cancelling out, either."

"I'm sure he didn't."

"Anyway, our relationship has become important to me. I care about you. You've been good to me tonight and I want to return the favor."

"But it's my job to be good to you. I'm the host of this ongoing party and you're my guest. I don't expect my guest to go down on me."

"Not even if she wants to?"

"Not even then. We have one more night of our arrangement. After that, the experiment will end and I'll no longer be the host. You'll no longer be my guest."

"And then you'll let me give you a—"

"That depends on a whole lot of things."

"Like the wedding, I guess. I'll be tied up Friday night with the rehearsal and the rehearsal dinner. I don't suppose Badger expects you to go to that."

"Actually, he does. I'll be there."

"You will? That's wonderful! Then at that point Ryker will find out about you."

"Yep."

"He's going to be so surprised."

"Yes, he will." He had plenty to figure out between now and then. When to tell her the truth. How to tell her the truth. He gazed down at her, his heart full. "I care about you, too."

"I know you do."

"One more kiss, and then we'll head back."

"Okay."

He settled down with ease of familiarity. His lips knew the contours of hers very well, now. Even so, the rush of emotion when he made the connection grew stronger with every kiss.

This one, more potent than all the others, simmered with the wonder of intimate touches and the splendor of her climax. The heat built faster now that he knew where it could lead.

Sooner than he would have liked, he lifted his mouth from hers and gulped for air. "We…need to…go."

"Yeah." She was breathing as hard as he was and her fingertips dug into the muscles of his shoulders. "I want you out of those jeans."

"Not happening. Where's your jacket?"

"Beside me somewhere."

He reached over, swept the area with one hand and found it. "I'll put this over you and go start the truck's heater. It's way colder than it was when we got here."

"Is it? I can't tell."

"You will once I move." He lifted away from her.

She sucked in a breath. "You're right."

He quickly spread the jacket over her. "Wait here."

"You know what? I'll just put on my stuff and come with you. I'm not some fragile flower."

"I know." He gave her a quick kiss. "Humor me and stay here. I like playing the hero."

"For the record, you do it well."

"Thanks." Grabbing his shirt, jacket and phone, he hopped to the ground. Good thing he'd called a halt. The moon was up. By Saturday night it would be full, so by now it was already bright enough to make the flashlight unnecessary. He had the truck running and the heater on in no time.

Leaving his jacket on the seat, he pulled his shirt over his head and tugged on his cap before he walked back to the tailgate. She'd stayed where he'd left her. Touching.

He pulled himself back up and sat beside her. "Time to go."

She turned her head toward him but made no move to get up. "The moon's arrived."

"I noticed."

"We should come out here sometime and stargaze for real. This is an awesome spot for it."

He glanced up. "It is. I even have a telescope."

"You do? I've always wanted one, but then I end up buying a new lens for my camera, instead. Now I really want to come out here with you and your telescope."

"Let's plan on it."

"After the wedding." She sat up.

He helped her on with the jacket. "Right, after the wedding. Zip up. I'll search for your bra and shirt." He crawled around behind her. "Found 'em."

"I like being with you, Raven. No matter what we're doing. You're easy to be with."

He sat back on his heels and gazed at her. "So are you. Being with you just feels right."

She nodded. "Badger knew what he was doing, didn't he?"

"Guess so." He handed over her bra and shirt and vaulted out of the truck bed. "Scoot over here and I'll lift you down."

"And carry me to the front of the truck?"

"Sure, why not?"

"I'm kidding!"

"I'm not." Once she was close to the edge, he scooped her into his arms and carted her, despite her protests, around to the passenger side. "Get the door, please."

Leaning over, she opened it and he deposited her inside. "Now tell me that wasn't big fun."

She laughed. "It was big fun. Thanks for the lift."

He smiled as he walked back and closed the tailgate. If only things could stay like this, light and breezy, enjoying each other's company, deepening the connection. But he was coming to the breaking point. And they both had a wedding to attend.

When he swung into the driver's seat, she was in the process of fastening her bra. Even in the dark, that shadowy motion was obvious, a woman arching her back and reaching behind it to fasten the hooks. Sexy move. "Need help?"

"Got it, but thanks." She put her arms in the sleeves of her shirt and pulled it up over her shoulders. "Do you want to look at those pictures when we get back?"

"I've been thinking about that. Considering where we are with each other, I doubt I could calmly hang out with you in the house without...."

"So how do you want to handle it?"

What he wanted and what he could live with were completely different options. He chose the latter. "I'll walk you to your Jeep and then run in and fetch your laptop. We'll look at the pictures another time."

"If you're worried about being in the house with me, then what's the plan for tomorrow night?"

"I'm working on it."

"But you still want me to come over?"

"Absolutely. I could always forget the shaving. I won't kiss you with that scouring pad on my face. That was my plan for tonight, in fact, but at the last minute I couldn't stand it."

"So you didn't exactly forget."

"Nope."

She hesitated. "Look, I don't want to make you uncomfortable, but if there's some issue, like a medical problem, I'm sure we can—"

"No medical problem." Sheesh. Didn't want her going *there*. "No psychological hang-ups, either. I'm a fully functioning, healthy male. It's just—"

"Do you think you'd be taking advantage of me?"

"In a way."

"Then let me put your mind at ease. You wouldn't be." Her voice was gentle. "I'd gladly give up my guest status."

He took a shaky breath. "I'll think about it." Only one scenario made sense. No way could he let her discover the truth at the rehearsal. That would be unfair to her and everyone there.

That left only one option.

_12_

Caitlin drove to the last scheduled meeting with Raven in a state of agitation. Something was bugging him, an issue significant enough that he'd draw the line when it came to his own sexual satisfaction. Why would he deny himself that? And deny them both the joy of mutual pleasure?

He'd said it wasn't a medical or psychological problem. She believed him. Then what could possibly stand in the way of an activity with the potential to be wonderful?

He'd made the case that she was his guest and his job was to please her, not vice-versa. But if she was willing to change that dynamic, why wasn't he? Nothing made sense.

Must have something to do with this experiment he and Badger had cooked up. Theoretically she wasn't supposed to learn about it until tomorrow.

Funny that she'd looked forward to finding out what the mystery was all about. Now she wasn't so sure she wanted to know. Raven had made several cryptic comments about it, as if she might not be happy with the outcome.

The experiment came to an end tonight. Was their relationship coming to an end, too? That seemed impossible after all they'd shared—the funny moments and the hot ones. Surely they'd go on seeing each other, right?

She parked in front of the house as always, but something was different about the place. What was it? *The lights.* Instead of glowing faintly, they were shining as brightly as those in the windows of the neighboring houses.

Had he decided to test whether his aviators would be enough eye protection for the rehearsal and the wedding? That made sense, except that he wouldn't need to do it while she was here.

Maybe the bright lights were designed to destroy the cozy, seductive atmosphere they'd enjoyed. Kissing wasn't as easy when someone wore sunglasses. Maybe he'd chosen the unshaven route, too, and didn't plan to kiss her at all, let alone invite her back to his bedroom.

If that was his plan, she wouldn't leave until he explained himself. He might claim to have no hang-ups, but something was going on with him and she'd find out what it was before she drove away tonight. Enough of the mysterious evasions.

Striding up the walk, she mounted the steps and pushed the doorbell. Raven would answer her questions tonight if she had to—

The door opened.

She blinked. Couldn't be. This was some bizarre dream. In a second she'd wake up and—

"Hello, Caitlin."

Raven's voice. Raven's broad shoulders. Raven's mouth and freshly shaven jaw. She gulped. "I don't...what..."

"Come on in. I know it's a shock. But I couldn't figure out an easier—"

"You're...you're..." Air. She desperately needed air.

"I'm Aaron. My pilot name is Raven. Seriously, come in. You look like you're ready to pass out. I'll get you some water."

"This can't be happening."

"Come inside." He reached for her arm.

She pulled it back. "Don't touch me."

Pain flashed in his eyes. His *golden* eyes. "Okay. But I'm begging you to come inside. You can yell at me. Punch me if you want. Just don't go back to your Jeep and leave. You're too upset to—"

"Don't you *dare* tell me what I can and can't do!"

"I wasn't..." He sighed. "Let me have it, then."

She took a breath as fury grew like a mushroom cloud in her chest. She opened her mouth. No telling what would come out. She didn't care.

From somewhere down the street, a car door closed, followed by laughter and cheerful conversation. She closed her mouth again. Screaming curses on his front porch wasn't her style, anyway. "I'll come in. Move back. *Way* back."

He held up both hands as he edged away from the door. "Take all the space you need."

"There's not enough space in the universe for us to coexist, buster." She stomped inside, closed the door and turned to face him, arms crossed over her chest. "Start. Talking."

"Want me to take your jacket?"

"No." Her stomach churned. He was even wearing the same damn shirt he'd had on the first night. To think that she'd kissed him. And last night...oh, God, she'd—

"Can I get you something? A beer? Glass of water?"

"No."

"Would you like to sit down, at least?"

"*No*. I want *answers*, buddy-boy."

Taking a shaky breath, he ran his fingers through his hair and gazed at her. Misery shone in his eyes. "I'm sorry."

"As well you should be! What the *hell* were you thinking?"

"That I had absolutely no chance with you."

Her bark of laughter surprised her. "Wrong."

"What?"

"You're in much deeper shit than that. You've descended to the *no way in hell, not if you were the last man on Earth* category. I'd rather spend time with a geriatric platypus with an overbite than hang out with—hey! Are you *laughing?*"

He ducked his head and scrubbed a hand over his face. Then he cleared his throat. When he looked at her again, all trace of humor was gone. His jaw tightened. "I'll miss everything about you, but most of all I'll miss the fun we've had."

"Fake fun."

"Was it?"

"You weren't who you said you were. That makes everything that happened a lie." The sharp edge of betrayal sliced into her heart. "How could you?"

"Like I said, I faced an insurmountable obstacle. You hated my name, so I changed it."

"And made up stuff!"

"Exaggerated a little."

"A *little*? Clearly there's nothing wrong with your eyes!"

"They're still sensitive. I wear the aviators whenever I'm outdoors and—"

"No, you don't! I just remembered something. Ryker's wedding was outside and you did *not* wear shades."

"Toughed it out, kept my Stetson pulled low. Shades seemed inappropriate for a groomsman at a wedding."

"Oh!" She snapped her fingers. "Wedding! I just figured out why tonight's the big reveal. Why the *experiment* had to end tomorrow. The rehearsal!"

"Right."

"That *sucks*. I have no choice but to be in your vicinity for the whole shebang. Wonderful."

"That's why yelling at me now would be a good idea. Call me every name in the book. Then maybe by tomorrow, you'll—"

"Want to boil your privates in hot oil?"

He winced.

"By tomorrow, I'll have had many, many minutes to obsess over this travesty and I'll be using every single one to dream up ways to torture you. If you think I'm furious now, just wait. You ain't seen nuthin' yet."

His chest heaved. "I'm sorry. That sounds lame, I know."

The stupid man still had a gorgeous body, damn him. "Lame doesn't even begin to cover it."

"I should never have tried this, but Badger—"

"*Badger.* Your partner in crime." A lump of disappointment lodged in her chest. Badger had betrayed her, too.

"He was only trying to help."

"Help trick me?" Her throat hurt.

"Help me find a solu—"

"He's lucky he's getting married day after tomorrow. I won't rip him a new one when he's—does Hayley know?"

"Only Badger and me."

"That's something, anyway. I'd hate to think—"

"I'm totally responsible for this. Blame me, not Badger."

"Badger's no innocent bystander."

"He was shocked about me kissing you."

"You *told* him?"

"You told him you had feelings for me!"

"Because I was gullible enough to believe your story!" Damn, it hurt. She'd been such a fool. "Was *any* of it true?"

"All of it, basically."

"Oh, really? Were you wounded?"

"Yes."

"Decorated for valor?"

"Yes."

She skewered him with a glare that should have set him on fire. "Were you having a problem *acclimating to civilian life*?"

"Well..."

"Aha! Big fat lie designed to prey on my tender heart."

"To soften your heart! I was hoping you'd see—"

"How clever you are? How easily you can seduce little ol' me?"

"No! Never! The point was—"

"Who came up with this brilliant con, you or Badger?"

"Doesn't matter. I'm to blame."

"Badger did, then."

"I didn't say that."

"No, but you didn't claim it was your idea, either. You would have if you were the architect. You'd want to protect him. You're loyal to the guy. I'll give you that."

"I—"

"But you really screwed up. I mean epically screwed up."

"Yeah." He scrubbed his fingers through his hair again.

"And if you think I'll keep my mouth shut for the next two days, you have another think—"

"Spread it around as much as you want."

"Don't worry. I will."

"Badger's expecting to hear from you. I told him I was telling you tonight."

Her breath caught. "Did you mention anything about...last night?"

"No." He swallowed. "That's between you and me."

"Between *Raven* and me." Her throat tightened. Pressure built behind her eyes. Uh-oh. She was losing it. "I have to go."

"Don't go. We haven't—"

"I'm outta here." She dashed for the door, flung it open and ran out.

"Caitlin!" He came after her.

The thump of his boots hitting the wooden porch and steps threw her into panic mode. "Don't follow me!" She yanked her keys from her pocket.

"I'm worried about you driving!"

Faster. Panting, she rounded the Jeep and jerked open the driver's door. When she tried to close it, he blocked it with his body.

"Stay here until you've calmed down. Please."

Dragging in air, she dredged up every ounce of willpower she possessed and glanced up at him. Pride calmed her voice. "I won't get in a wreck. I can't. People are counting on me for the next two days. I won't disappoint them."

He held her gaze. Dark fire gleamed in his golden eyes. "Okay." He moved back.

She closed the door. Getting the key in the ignition was a trick. She finally managed to start the engine and pull away. She didn't look in the rearview mirror. He'd be standing in the street, watching her.

She didn't want that image haunting her during what would be a very long night.

_13_

Tailspin. Aaron texted the word to Badger, not knowing whether he'd be looking at his phone. The guy was on the brink of a wedding extravaganza he'd anticipated for more than eighteen months. He had better things to do than keep track of Aaron's drama.

Despite that, Badger texted back within two minutes. *Be right there.*

Aaron quickly replied that driving over wasn't necessary. Badger didn't respond.

Five minutes later his red truck appeared in front of the house. Aaron walked out to greet him. "You didn't have to do this."

"I think I did." He held up a six-pack. "I purely hate to see a man drinkin' alone."

"Maybe I'd decide not to drink."

"That's as likely as a Southerner givin' up his deep-fat fryer." He gestured with the six-pack. "Proceed. These are gettin' warm."

Aaron turned and started back into the house. "Shouldn't you be with Hayley?"

"I'll be with Hayley for the rest of my life." Badger followed him up the steps. "I explained that you had a crisis goin' on, and she practically pushed me out the door. She likes you, for some reason or other."

"She might not after she hears about this fiasco. Did you tell her?"

"Not yet."

"She might not care for either of us after she finds out what we've been up to. If Caitlin is anything to go by, our actions aren't going to play well with the women of Eagles Nest. Probably won't go over well with the guys, either." He walked into the living room.

Badger came in, closed the door and handed him the beer. "Stick these in the fridge and rustle up whatever munchies you got. I'm buildin' us a fire."

"Don't be shy. Make yourself right at home."

"I'm takin' charge because you're in shock. You may not realize it, but—"

"Caitlin's in shock, too."

"Would you prefer I take this beer over to her place?"

"I don't think you'd be welcome."

"Exactly. I'm givin' aid and comfort where I can."

"Do you think she'll call anybody? I hate to think of her sitting in her place dealing with this by herself."

Badger gazed at him and sighed. "What you're sayin' is that I need to call Hayley and tell her the deets. I'd prefer not explainin' it over the phone, but—"

"I never mentioned Hayley. Why would you call her?"

Badger shook his head. "You have so much to learn. I'm callin' her so she can go over and check on Caitlin while I'm proppin' you up. A team effort."

"Oh."

"Considerin' the poor timin', it'll be yet another test of my relationship with my bride-to-be. This is the kind of news best delivered in person."

"Then don't call her."

"And leave Caitlin sitting alone in her apartment?"

"Maybe she'll call someone."

"Think about it. We're on the eve of a big weekend involvin' most of the community. Is she really goin' to contact somebody about her personal issues tonight, of all nights?"

"Good point."

"I'll take one of those beers before you put them away. To grease the wheels before I call Hayley."

He handed over one of the bottles. "We never should have started this."

"That's cryin' over spilled milk, good buddy." He twisted the top off and took a swig of the beer. "We've spilled that milk." He handed Aaron the cap. "Now we have to clean it up."

"I'm not sure we can. She went nuclear on me."

"Which means we have us a challenge." He grinned. "And I do love me a challenge."

"Badger! This isn't a game."

"That's where you're wrong. It's the best kind of game. Nobody needs to go trudgin' home empty-handed. You can both win. All you have to do is stay loose and have fun."

"For your information, I'm not having fun and neither is she."

"That's a cryin' shame, because your Raven gig was hysterical."

"Tell that to her."

"I will if I get the chance. You goin' to put that beer away? It's best to keep it at a constant temperature."

"You sound concerned."

"I am."

"Isn't that a contradiction? What about staying loose?"

"It's simple. Play at life." He smiled and lifted the bottle. "But take your beer seriously."

Aaron gazed at him and shook his head. "I can't decide if you're a genius or a crackpot."

"Not a lot of difference between the two. Now get out of here. I need privacy for makin' this delicate phone call to my darlin'."

"Give me a holler when you're done." He headed into the kitchen with the beer. The situation was still dire, but not as horrific as it had been before Badger arrived.

After grabbing a beer for himself, he refrigerated the rest. He tucked the carton next to the one he'd bought today in anticipation of exactly this kind of fustercluck. Too bad his hunch had been right on.

Twisting off the cap, he took a long swallow from the bottle that likely would be the first of several. Then he leaned against the counter and gazed at the label. McGavin's Pale Ale. All the rage. A natural to serve Caitlin. And now, every time he drank the stuff...

To hell with it. He chugged it and took another bottle from the fridge. Badger's soft murmur drifted in from the living room. Given the timing, expecting Hayley to abandon her evening plans to go see Caitlin was a big ask.

The murmurs ceased and Badger appeared in the kitchen, phone in hand. "God, I love that woman."

"She'll do it?"

"She's goin' to text her first, and if Caitlin doesn't want her to come over, she'll respect that. But if she says okay, then—" He paused as his phone pinged. "Good deal. Caitlin gave her the green light."

Aaron exhaled. "I owe Hayley big time."

"Oh, she'll be collectin' from both of us for this deal. She knew I was up to somethin', but she thought it was tied in with the bagpipes."

"A man of many secrets."

"Fortunately, she cherishes that little quirk. And she even gets why we did this."

"She's not upset?"

"Can't very well be upset considerin' we ran a fake fiancée con on her mom year before last. Hayley's the perfect person to talk with Caitlin tonight." He glanced at the empty beer bottle on the counter. "I see one dead soldier but no sign of munchies."

"Right. Munchies." He pushed away from the counter. "I'll—"

"Let me do it. Just keep on drinkin'." He got out a couple of bowls and pulled bags of chips and pretzels out of the cupboard. "I spotted a sweet deal on a Cirrus Vision SF50 today."

"A jet?"

"Yeah, baby." He dumped chips in one bowl and pretzels in the other. "Tell me you wouldn't love havin' a jet in the lineup."

"Hell, yes. Can we afford it?"

"Luke says we can and we need the deduction. I love havin' a brother-in-law—well, as of Saturday he'll be official—who encourages us to expand. Have you looked at the books lately?"

"Nope."

"Badger Air is makin' money hand-over-fist." He picked up the bowls. "If you'll grab my beer—"

"Got it." He followed Badger into the living room.

"Luke's advised us to raise all our salaries." He set the bowls on the table and sat in the chair Aaron had taken each night. "We can afford to do that *and* get us a jet."

"Nice." He settled down in Caitlin's chair. Could he still smell her perfume? Nah. Overactive imagination.

"You could take Caitlin up in it."

"Oh, sure." He grabbed some chips. "She'd rather hang out with a geriatric platypus with an overbite than spend time with me."

Badger cracked up. "She said that?"

"Uh-huh."

"Gotta love a woman who comes up with a creative line under pressure."

"Made me laugh. Which she did *not* appreciate."

"It's a good sign that she's ticked. It means she's emotionally involved. You got your foot in the door, like we hoped."

"She slammed it shut, too. Hurts like a sonofabitch."

"But you got to kiss her. I surely didn't anticipate that happenin' when we set this up."

"Me, either. But things just...escalated."

"You didn't say what went on last night."

"Don't plan to, either."

"Oh, hey, that sounds promisin'. Kissin', followed by *more* than kissin'. You're in a way stronger position than I figured on."

"Doesn't feel like it. You didn't see how mad she was. She mentioned boiling my privates in hot oil."

"At least she's thinkin' about your privates."

"Nice try."

"Work with me, here. She deployed the words *hot* and *oil* in that sentence. On the surface, it sounds threatenin', but underneath there's a whole other message goin' on."

"Like what?"

"She wants you bad."

Aaron laughed. "Sure she does. Let's go with that." He gulped more beer. "What are the specs on this jet we're buying?"

"Before we get into jet talk, I need to say somethin'."

"Go for it." He was developing a nice buzz.

"You could be blamin' me for talkin' you into this. But you're not."

He gazed into the fire and sipped his beer. "Truth is, I'm grateful."

"Grateful that it blew up in your face?"

"I'll admit tonight was hell. But those other three nights were heaven. It's highly likely she'll refuse to have anything more to do with me, but at least I had that much."

"That's sportin' of you, but I still think you have a—"

"I'm not counting on anything, Badger. And I'm done whining about the way it turned out. I'd do it all again, even knowing how it would end."

"Wow. You're in deep, good buddy."

"I am, and you know what? That's okay. I was right about her. Without you and your wacky plan, I always would have wondered." He lifted his beer in his friend's direction. "Thanks."

__14__

Caitlin was furious with Badger, but she wasn't about to let that anger ruin her budding friendship with Hayley, who'd had nothing to do with the episode. Shooting the couple's engagement pictures earlier in the year had been a blast and she'd invited Hayley to have lunch with her whenever they could work it out.

That had gone so well that they'd continued to meet for lunch or coffee whenever their busy schedules permitted. Because Hayley's dad was a minister and Caitlin's had been career military, they shared a history of being uprooted as children.

Eagles Nest had become the hometown Caitlin had always wished for and she wanted to create lasting friendships here. Hayley was a good start.

The front window gave her a view of the street so she could watch for visitors. When Hayley's compact sedan pulled up in front of the building, Caitlin hurried downstairs to open the front door. Hayley commuted to Bozeman five days a week and was one of the few people in town besides Caitlin who didn't drive a truck.

She came in and gathered Caitlin into a tight hug. "Men. Can't live with 'em, can't live without 'em."

"Ain't that the truth." Caitlin stepped back with a shaky smile. "Come on upstairs. I have wine and chocolate."

"My favorites." She followed Caitlin up the stairs and accepted a glass of red wine before settling in one of the barrel chairs grouped around a coffee table.

Caitlin took the lid off a large box of dark chocolate truffles and set the box on the table. "I must be psychic. I bought this last week and never opened it."

"I'm surprised you didn't start in on it the minute you got home."

"I was so upset I didn't think of it. I was too busy punching pillows." She settled in a chair facing Hayley. "I *so* appreciate that you came over, considering all the other things you could be doing tonight."

"Don't worry about that. I'd be obsessing over last-minute details just like my mother is right now. I texted her I'd be out of pocket for the next couple of hours so we won't be interrupted."

"What if something critical comes up?"

"It won't. She won't allow it." She leaned forward. "You really didn't guess it was Aaron?"

"Nope. I've asked myself a thousand times how I could have been fooled. In my defense, I haven't spent much time with the guy. I could tell he liked me and since I'd never date him, staying away seemed kinder."

"Okay, you didn't know him well." Hayley finished a piece of chocolate and picked up her wine glass. "But their gonzo story about a vet named Raven slipping into town unannounced and moving into Aaron's house...didn't that seem odd?"

"You need to read the letter he wrote." She walked over to a small desk in the corner and picked it up. "I almost ripped it to shreds when I came home, but I'm glad I didn't, because it's a valuable piece of evidence. And a masterpiece." She handed it to Hayley.

She read quickly. "Damn, it *is* good. I recognize Badger's wording in some of it, but the handwriting is Aaron's. It's neater than usual. I wonder how many tries it took to produce this."

"I hope they both sweated bullets over it."

"I'll bet they did. This must have been why Badger went over to Aaron's on Sunday night. He said something about making sure Aaron was okay because he'd overindulged at Saturday's bachelor bash."

"Is Aaron a big drinker?"

"Nah. I'm sure Badger exaggerated so he'd have an excuse to help him craft this letter. I see why you fell for it. He even drew a raven at the bottom."

"Yep. I thought that was adorable." She rolled her eyes.

"You've never heard Ryker or Badger call him Raven?"

"Not that I remember. Like I said, I tried to maintain some distance. You know when a guy looks at you a certain way, you can tell he wants to ask you out?"

"Sure. And Aaron's pretty transparent." She took a deep breath. "At least he used to be. He must have put on the performance of his life."

"Maybe that's another reason I didn't guess. He doesn't seem like the type to do something like this."

"He's not. I guess he was desperate and Badger…well, being Badger…"

"Did you know Aaron had a crush on me?"

"Suspected it. Then Badger confirmed it. Aaron told him you were the only woman in Eagles Nest he had any interest in dating."

"That's ridiculous. There are lots of wonderful women in this town."

"But only one Caitlin Dempsey. Badger said he wouldn't shut up about you. Raved about your creativity, your dedication, your sense of humor. He also thinks you're hot."

An unwelcome warmth invaded her core. She ignored it and took a swallow of wine. "I suppose I should be flattered."

"I'm not making excuses for him. For either of them. What they did was wrong."

"Damn right it was. You should have seen the setup. Two easy chairs pulled up to a cozy fire, a couple of bottles of McGavin's Pale Ale, dim lights because supposedly he couldn't tolerate normal brightness. They thought of everything."

"Badger told me about the cap and the scruff. But even so, it seems amazing that you weren't able to recognize—"

"I didn't because I desperately wanted to believe Raven's touching story. You read the letter. I bought the premise. Hook, line and sinker."

"And you liked Raven?"

"Yes." Hard to admit.

"Were you attracted to him?"

Even harder to admit. "Yes, damn it, I was!" She hid her warm face in her hands and took a deep breath. "I thought he was sexy and mysterious." She met Hayley's compassionate gaze.

"That's what they wanted you to think."

"And boy, did I fall right in with the plan. No last name? No problem. After all, having only one name is cool, right? I turned him into effing *Zorro*."

She chuckled. "Oh, Caitlin."

"I cringe to think of how I played right into his hands." *Literally.* "I came up with explanations for the screwy stuff. When he fed me the BS that Aaron had three night flights in a row, which is why he was never there, I praised Aaron for selflessly volunteering so Ryker and Badger could spend their evenings at home with their sweethearts."

"Man, you really did want to believe."

"My dad and brother served with distinction. I'm such a sucker for the story of a wounded hero who's sacrificed years in service to his country."

"Which, to be fair, is true."

"Tonight he said it was, but he also admitted they exaggerated some things."

"Not that part. Aaron broke his leg when the plane he and Ryker were flying was shot down behind enemy lines. The bones took forever to heal. Several operations in a German hospital. Lots of PT."

She shivered. "They were captured?"

"Rescued in the nick of time. You could ask Ryker about it. On second thought, ask Kendra. Ryker doesn't like to talk about it."

"Kendra must not like to talk about it either. I've spent quite a bit of time with her since I moved here and she's never—"

"Yeah, you're right. It's not a favorite topic in that family. I wouldn't know if Badger hadn't filled me in on the details. Ryker never planned to tell Kendra about the crash."

"Really?"

"He lived, so he didn't see the point in giving her the grisly details. She only found out when Aaron's mom wrote her a letter praising Ryker for saving her beloved son's life."

Her stomach hollowed out. She was ready to kill him, but if he'd died... "So Aaron really does have a mom in Ohio?"

"Sure does."

"He said she taught him to waltz."

"It's true he can waltz, but I didn't know his mother taught him. She's coming out here next month. I'm eager to meet her."

"You like him, don't you?"

"At the risk of irritating the hell out of you—yes, I like him. But I could jerk a knot in his tail—Badger's too—for what they pulled on you this week."

"It makes me feel stupid, and that's not a nice place to be."

"No, it isn't."

"Let me show you something else. I took a picture of Raven. Several, in fact."

"Oh, really?"

"Yeah." She went back to the desk for her laptop. Looking at those pictures would be torture, but Hayley needed to see what she'd been up against.

Searching for the images wasn't much fun, either. A beautiful, innocent moment in the romantic glow of the setting sun had been ruined.

She located them, brought the laptop to Hayley and knelt beside her chair. "This isn't a true test, because you already know it's him." Reaching over, she scrolled to her favorite sepia-toned one.

"Whoa. That's a very cool shot. I thought you guys were inside all the time."

"The autumn leaves in his yard are outstanding. I noticed them the first night and asked if I could bring my camera the second night. He came out while I was shooting."

"Badger has one of those jackets. I admit I have a thing for flyboys."

Her insides twisted. So did she. "Would you have instantly recognized him as Aaron?"

"If I didn't know it was, maybe not. Although I've seen him stand that way. They never lose that military bearing. Makes them look sort of cocky."

"Yeah." She sighed.

Hayley gave her a funny look.

"I mean, yes, so, so cocky. Think they're all that and a bag of chips."

"Right." She smiled and returned her attention to the picture. "The cap pulled low and the aviators disguise him fairly well. But where's the scruff?"

"The second night he shaved it off before I arrived."

"And you *still* didn't know it was Aaron?"

"I was so far into my fantasy I wasn't looking for any reason to doubt the story."

Hayley studied the picture. "I get it. Damn, he has it all going on. I see why you wanted to capture this image."

And why, before I took these, I kissed him. And later on, we kissed again, and again….

"So what are these others?"

"Huh?" Yikes. Caught dreaming of kisses. "Just more of the same. We don't have to go through them all." She reached for the laptop. "I just wanted you to get the idea."

"Oh, I do." Hayley closed it and gave it to her. "It was a well-baited trap. Most women would have reacted exactly the way you did."

"Thanks. Makes me feel better."

"Did you ever see his eyes?"

"Not until tonight." So many emotions reflected in that golden gaze—remorse and sorrow. A brief sparkle of laughter. And at the end, a blazing fire of determination when he'd tried to keep her from leaving.

"His eyes would have been a dead giveaway. They're such an interesting color."

"I suppose I would have recognized his eyes. But maybe not unless he took off his cap and looked straight at me. Even tonight, when he stood in the doorway, it took me several seconds to put it all together."

"That must have been a very tough moment."

"You have no idea." She picked up the wine bottle and refilled their glasses.

"So what now?"

"Good question." After taking a piece of chocolate, she sat down. "But rest assured this won't affect my work. You'll get my best effort for the next two days."

"I never doubted it. I'm just sorry you'll be forced to spend time with those two. It would be nice if you didn't have to see either of them for a while."

"Sure would. Why in hell would they pull this stunt the week before the wedding? That seems so—"

"I'm learning how Badger thinks. My guess is he figured they had a better chance of making it work while everyone was concentrating on something else."

"Okay, but Rav—I mean *Aaron*—told me the first night that I'd find out about their experiment by Friday. So they were always planning to drop this bombshell right before the big event."

"I did mention the lousy timing to Badger. He said they had no clue how this would turn out. For all they knew, you'd recognize Aaron the first night and it would have been over before it started."

"If only I had. Instead…"

"There was way more emotional involvement than he'd counted on. He used the term *runaway train*."

"Oh, God, it was, wasn't it?" She stared at Hayley. "Have you told anybody about this?"

"Of course not. I told Mom I'd be away from my phone for a while but I didn't say why."

"Aaron said I could tell anybody I wanted, spread it around. At the time that sounded like the perfect revenge. But I wasn't thinking straight. Gossip like that would affect your wedding."

Hayley sighed. "It would, and Badger deserves to suffer the consequences, but Luke and Abigail don't. My mother and dad don't."

"And *you* don't." Thank heavens she'd punched pillows instead of making phone calls. Disaster averted. "Only the four of us know about this. We need to keep it that way. At least for the next two days."

"I won't say anything."

"And I certainly won't. What about the guys?"

Hayley pulled her phone out of her purse. "Leave them to me." Her jaw tightened and her eyes flashed with an unholy fire. "You might want to cover your ears, though. I'm about to tell Badger how the cow eats the cabbage."

"Are you kidding?" Caitlin grinned. "I want to hear every single word."

* * *

Badger's truck was the only vehicle parked outside when Caitlin arrived at the renovated barn at three the next afternoon. The possibility that Aaron had come along had her stomach in a knot, but Badger was the only one in the building when she walked through the front door lugging her equipment.

She left it against the back wall and went to meet him. "Hey, Badger."

"I should have waited outside so I could help you with all that."

"No worries. I'm used to carting it around."

He took off his Stetson as he came toward her and placed it against his chest like a shield. "Caitlin, my deepest apologies for what you've suffered because of my actions. I talked Aaron into it. He had doubts from the get-go, but I can be very convincin' and he—"

"Save it, Badger. I spent three evenings with the man. You might have been the catalyst, but I can testify that he was all in. And for the record, he insisted on taking all the blame. Said you were a very small part of the operation."

"I was a major part, but he would take the heat because that boy is as loyal as a golden retriever. You won't find anyone more willin' to go the extra mile than—"

"So now he's a dog instead of a raven? I can't keep track of all his personas."

"I know this sticks in your throat like a hair in a biscuit, but I promise we didn't set out to hurt you."

Her throat tightened. "Maybe not, but you did, anyway."

"And for that, I'm sorrier than I can ever say. Aaron's even sorrier than that."

"Which you both should be."

"Yes, ma'am. Because of us, you likely had a miserable night's sleep."

"I slept well, thank you."

"Oh. That's…I'm glad to hear it."

"I'm fine, Badger." Not quite true, but giving Badger a hard time wasn't nearly as much fun as she wanted it to be. Hayley had done such a good job dressing him down over the phone last night that adding to that was like piling on. "We should get to work."

"Yes, ma'am. I'll show you what Virginia has in mind." As he put on his hat and moved briskly over to the control panel, he didn't act the least bit the worse for wear.

When Hayley had called the guys last night, they'd clearly decided to drown their sorrows in McGavin's Pale Ale. But Badger had a reputation for drinking everyone under the table and emerging fresh as a daisy the next day.

"How's…how's Aaron?"

Badger turned, his gaze steady. "What do you want to know?"

"Just if he's…you know what? Never mind. Let's see those lights."

__15__

Aaron's drive from his house to the wedding venue didn't take long enough. Before he was anywhere near ready to face Caitlin, he'd pulled into the parking lot. Her battered white Cherokee sat in the front row of spaces near the barn doors, which stood open. He chose a spot in the back.

This is for Badger and Hayley. The mantra had sustained him throughout a day spent regretting the numerous beers he'd consumed. They'd gone through Badger's six-pack and his.

He should have learned by now that trying to keep up with Badger was a recipe for disaster. But the guy drew people into the game because hanging out with him, drunk or sober, was so much fun.

Sometime around one in the morning, he'd insisted they had to waltz around the living room to prove that Aaron hadn't made that up. Naturally they hadn't completed the circuit without crashing into the furniture. Two drunk cowboys of their size and weight had far less margin for error than one focused cowboy and a slim, athletic photographer.

She was somewhere beyond those open doors, preparing to capture the precious moments of the rehearsal. Soon he'd share interior space with her.

He didn't know how she'd be. How he would be. He'd changed shirts four times and finally gone with his first choice, a black one with pearl snaps and gold piping on the yoke and collar.

Badger had sent him a text about fifteen minutes ago. *FYI, she asked about you.*

What was he supposed to do with that? Did she sincerely want to check on him or was she being polite? Did she hope to hear he was doing okay or was she fantasizing he'd been strangled by someone's pet python?

Probably the first thing, that he was okay. If she'd asked about him, she wanted to know that he was functioning and hadn't thrown himself off a cliff in despair. She cared about him. The depth of her concern was anybody's guess, though. After all, she had mentioned boiling his privates.

He climbed out of the truck wearing his aviators. His black Stetson lay brim-side up on the passenger seat. No hats during the rehearsal, but all the guys would have on their dress Stetsons during dinner and dancing at the Guzzling Grizzly.

The absence of a hat as he started toward the front door was unnerving. He missed the psychological cover it provided. He'd have to walk in bare-headed, the way he'd greeted Caitlin at the door last night. He'd have to take off the aviators, too. Nowhere to run, nowhere to hide.

He'd almost reached the open doorway when someone called his name. He turned as

Kendra and Quinn approached, all smiles. Would they be greeting him warmly if they knew about his shenanigans? Likely not.

"Nice shirt! You look great." Kendra gave him a quick kiss on the cheek.

"Thanks." He gave her a hug and shook hands with Quinn, who was also hatless. "I almost don't recognize you without your Stetson."

"No worries. It's in the truck waiting for me."

"Same here."

"A double wedding!" Kendra's blue eyes gleamed with excitement. "I've never been to one. Have you?"

"Can't say I have."

"It'll be unique," Quinn said. "Luke and Abigail insist they got rid of the skunk smell on Delilah, but I have my doubts they could do it that fast. Kendra offered to be their official smell tester this morning, but—"

"They said it wasn't necessary." She glanced at Aaron. "Which makes me suspect she still smells like skunk."

"Hope not. That would—"

"There's the missing groomsman." Ryker appeared in the open doorway. "Hey Mom, Dad. We're about ready, so come grab a seat. Aaron, you're with me."

"Yes, sir. On my way, sir." Aaron winked at Kendra and gestured for her to go in ahead of him with Quinn.

She flashed him a smile. As she walked through the doorway, she leaned toward Quinn and spoke in an undertone. "I still get a charge when he calls you Dad."

"Me, too."

Aaron's chest tightened. His father had died young, just like Ryker's. He was happy that Ryker and his brothers had Quinn, and, yeah, a little envious. A dad would be nice to have.

He tucked his aviators in his shirt pocket as he hurried after Ryker and scanned the room for Caitlin. There. On the far side of the room with Abigail and her best buds, Ingrid and Roxanne. All four women were making over Delilah in her wedding tux. Caitlin leaned down and scratched behind the border collie's ears. Then she glanced up at Abigail and smiled. His throat went dry. So beautiful.

He'd told her once. He should have said it way more than that. He'd had so many chances. Wasted them. She stood, reached for a camera lying on a pew and focused it on Delilah.

"Raven? You coming, man?"

"Yeah." He tore his attention away and put his feet in motion. "Kendra was talking about the skunk thing. Does Delilah still smell?"

"There's debate about that. Okay, Badger, Raven's here. Does Hayley still want him to meet her maid of honor before we start?"

"She does." Badger flashed him the usual confident grin. "She's over yonder with Hayley." He tilted his head toward the far side of the room.

"I see." The two stood—of course—only about ten feet away from Caitlin's group.

Badger glanced at him. "How's it hangin', good buddy?"

"I'm doing okay, bridegroom."

"Then let's go meet Sheila. She finally arrived about two hours ago." He ambled in that direction.

"Cutting it close." Aaron fell into step beside him.

"Plane malfunction. She got stuck overnight in Chicago."

"Rotten luck."

"For her." Badger slowed and lowered his voice. "For us, it was a blessin'. I couldn't have asked Hayley to do that little favor if Sheila had flown in yesterday like expected."

"How are things with Hayley?"

"She vented most of her frustration with me during our phone conversation last night. So we're good, but I'm scared to drink. Might loosen my tongue."

"That would be bad."

"Can't imagine goin' on the wagon at this particular time, though. It bein' my weddin' and all."

"Yeah, but if you let something slip when you're toasted…"

"She'll cream my corn." He glanced in Hayley's direction and raised his voice. "Darlin', you ladies got a minute?"

"Absolutely." She smiled at Aaron as they approached. "Hey, you." Only a slight flicker in her eyes indicated she wasn't totally glad to see him.

"Hey, gorgeous." He gave her a quick hug.

She hugged him back and murmured *you're an idiot* in his ear.

"Duly noted." Then he turned on the charm as she introduced him to Sheila something-or-other. With Caitlin in his peripheral vision, he had trouble concentrating on anyone else.

Sheila was much more focused. "Aaron Donahue." She clasped his hand in a firm grip. "I know a guy with that exact name."

"Doesn't everybody? I had no idea it was so common. It's the new John Smith."

She laughed. "The one I know isn't as funny as you."

"Likely a lot more handsome, though."

"I wouldn't say that, either."

She was flirting with him. Badger gave him a nudge, clearly a signal this was a golden opportunity to show Caitlin that other women found him attractive. He didn't give a damn whether Caitlin understood that or not. She wasn't the type to be influenced by such things.

Badger loyally steered the conversation in his direction and threw in comments designed to make him look good. *Crackerjack pilot. Great dancer. Nobody can waltz like this guy*—all spoken loud enough to reach Caitlin in case she might be listening.

He appreciated Badger's effort, so he played along as best he could. Joking around with Hayley's friend wasn't easy when his focus was on the sweet lilt of Caitlin's voice as she took pictures of Delilah and talked with her friends.

"Hey, troops!" Ryker's commanding voice carried without benefit of a mic. "Let's get this show on the road! Groomsmen, front and center. Ladies, to the back of the room, please."

"Looks like Cowboy's gettin' serious." Badger glanced over his shoulder before turning back to the women. "It's been a pleasure talkin' with you, ladies." He gave Aaron another nudge.

"Sure has." Movement off to his left distracted him. Caitlin had stopped taking pictures. She was looking directly at him. He forced himself to keep his attention on Hayley's maid of honor. "Nice meeting you, Shirley."

"Sheila."

"*Sheila.* Right, sorry. I should be able to remember that. I have a cousin named Sheila."

She grinned and repeated his line. "Doesn't everybody? Save me a dance tonight, okay?"

"You bet." He figured she walked away with Hayley after that, although he was too distracted to say for sure. An unsmiling Caitlin was coming straight for him.

"Bogie at ten o'clock," Badger said under his breath.

"I see her."

"I'll be leavin', now."

"Coward."

"Facilitator." Badger squeezed his shoulder and left.

Aaron stood alone. And waited.

Caitlin's blue gaze was troubled and a small frown line creased the space between her eyebrows.

His doing. All his doing. He swallowed. "Hi."

"Hi." She took a breath. "I just thought it would be good if we spoke to each other. Broke the ice."

He nodded. "Good idea. Ice can be damned slippery." He worked hard to breathe without gasping. "How are you?"

"Okay. You?"

"Okay."

"I heard Sheila say she knows somebody with your name."

His eyes widened. "You don't think that's your—"

"Oh, no, heavens no. She lives in New Jersey. My ex is a California surfer dude. I doubt he's ever been to the East Coast."

"Surfer, huh?" He'd never thought one way or another about surfers until now. Who did they think they were, anyway, riding their boards half-naked, showing off their muscles? Irritating as hell.

"Turns out your response to Sheila is right. Your name is like the one-thousandth most common name in the country."

"You're kidding."

"Look it up."

"I believe you."

"Raven! Need you over here!"

"Coming!" He gazed into her eyes. "Gotta go."

"Me, too. I just wanted—"

"I appreciate it." He sucked in a breath. "See you." He turned and made tracks for his spot in the lineup. He wasn't sure what that was all about, but at least she was talking to him. And evidently looking up his name.

_16_

Caitlin's attitude toward Aaron hadn't changed. She was still angry with him for tricking her and she didn't like his name any better than she ever had. But Sheila's interest annoyed her. She wasn't proud of that reaction, but there it was.

It stuck in her craw that he'd been paying attention to some interloper from Jersey when he was supposed to be crazy about *her* damn it. Even if she didn't want him.

How jacked up was that? She partly blamed the black shirt. She'd watched for him to come in because she hadn't wanted him to catch her by surprise. Coming face-to-face with him without warning could be a disaster.

If she responded inappropriately—yelping or jumping away, she'd attract unwanted attention. Keeping this secret required vigilance over her emotions for the next two days.

He'd been one of the last to arrive, which wasn't surprising. He had to be as nervous about seeing her again as she was about seeing him. Then he'd walked in, sexy aviators on and wearing a striking black shirt that molded to his torso and showed off his pecs.

The gold piping was a great touch and emphasized his broad shoulders. When he'd finally made his way to her side of the room, she'd managed to confirm that the piping brought out the gold flecks in his eyes.

No wonder Sheila had wanted to eat him up with a spoon. Had he always been that good looking? Logically, the answer had to be yes. She just hadn't allowed herself to notice.

Now that she was hypersensitive to his presence, she grudgingly admitted that whether he called himself Raven or Aaron, he was hot. So what? He was still the guy who'd perpetrated a hoax to further his own selfish agenda. Not nice.

And his name—at least most of the time—was Aaron Donahue. It might rank one thousandth in popularity with the rest of the country, but it was her least favorite name of all.

Speaking with him briefly had lowered her stress level and demonstrated that she could hold a conversation without wanting to smack him. Good thing she'd calmed down. Virginia's new lighting required all her concentration. She had to adjust her settings constantly.

But meeting the challenge proved to be the invigorating task she needed, and these folks deserved her best. Being chosen as the photographer for this epic event was a privilege she didn't take lightly.

She'd worked with Virginia on many events, but none as important as this. Virginia had given her all to provide a grand occasion for her son and daughter as they wed their chosen mates.

Her husband Warren had worked with each couple to craft memorable vows.

Their loving efforts put her own drama in perspective. By the end of the rehearsal, she'd mellowed out. She could even smile at herself for being annoyed by Sheila.

As members of the wedding party started filtering out of the building, Badger came over to ask if she needed help packing up.

"Thanks, but most of this stays here. I'll just take a small camera bag over to the GG since all you want are candid shots."

He nodded. "How do you think it went with the lights?"

"It was fun. I thought it might turn out to be frustrating, but I had a good time experimenting. I think I have some interesting stuff. I'll know better after I start editing."

"When will you be doin' that?"

"Probably in the morning. I'm not sure I'll be up to it tonight."

"You're a hard workin' woman." Regret softened his gaze. "Ashamed to say I didn't consider I was takin' advantage of your valuable time when I…"

"Set me up?" She murmured the words, because a few people remained in the building.

He grimaced. "Yes, ma'am. I've been an inconsiderate bastard. I've been tryin' to think of what I can do to make amends."

"I'm sure you'll come up with something."

"Here's one idea. Aaron told me last night that you'd like to use Badger Air for some senior portraits. Then again, you might've changed your mind, considerin'—"

"Oh, no, I'd love to use that location. I was planning to ask you if he didn't." She accepted that it would involve contact with Aaron. She wouldn't deprive the seniors of the opportunity just because she wanted to avoid him.

"That's good news. I'll clear it with Cowboy, but I can't imagine he'll object. You won't be charged anythin'."

"I doubt Ryker will go for letting me use your facility for free."

"He won't, but I'll pay it."

"Forever?"

"Well, uh—"

"I'm kidding. I'm not going to take advantage of your guilty conscience to shake you down. Ryker will probably ask for the same amount I give his mom for use of Wild Creek. I'll pay it and gladly."

"What if I cover the cost for a couple of years?"

"No, thanks. I'm not letting you off that easy."

He sighed. "Now you're soundin' like Hayley."

"That's a compliment. You've got a gem, there."

"Don't I know it. She's the—ah, here comes my future mother-in-law lookin' for her ride."

"How'd it go?" Virginia strolled over, elegant as always in a slinky navy outfit.

"Great, far as I can tell. I'll know better after I get a chance to go through what I have."

"Glad to hear it. Everyone's left but us chickens. Badger, you about ready?"

"Yes, ma'am. I wanted to make sure Caitlin didn't need any help gettin' packed up, but she says she doesn't need most of this stuff for the GG."

"She doesn't. Not when we'll all be going crazy with our phones."

"That's a fact. I guarantee we'll have more pictures than you can shake a stick at. And I'll bet Caitlin could use some time off."

"Don't worry about that, Badger." She was enjoying his contrite behavior, however. Sweet revenge.

"Great idea," Virginia said. "You should take some time off. Tomorrow will be way more intense." She glanced at Badger. "How about only having her shoot for thirty minutes or so tonight?"

"Works for me. Let me text the others. I'm sure they'll go along with it." He pulled out his phone and quickly typed a message.

"I'm happy to work longer, though. Just let me know." If they only wanted thirty minutes from her, she'd go home and edit. "I'm gonna head on over there, so I can get some shots before it gets too rambunctious." She reached for her camera bag.

"I'll take that to your Jeep for you." Badger looped the strap over his shoulder.

"Thanks." She'd be sure and let Hayley know he was groveling quite nicely.

Virginia followed them out and locked the massive barn doors. "Wasn't Delilah adorable in that tux?"

"She was," Caitlin said. "I got some great shots of her before the rehearsal started."

"Cowboy thinks she still smells," Badger said. "But I don't—there's my phone." He took it from his pocket and tapped the screen. "Everybody agrees. Thirty minutes tonight is plenty."

"Great. That'll give me a chance to go home and start editing what I just took."

"Go home and edit?" Virginia laid a hand on her arm. "I was hoping you'd stay. Kick up your heels a little. Relax."

"Oh." Relax with that black-shirt-wearing cowboy around? Not likely.

"You work so hard, honey." Virginia gave her arm a squeeze. "Why not take a break, eat some food, drink some beer and dance a little? Do you like to dance? I don't remember ever seeing you out there."

"I like to dance." She didn't dare look at Badger, who was busy studying the polished toes of his dress boots. "But I've been so busy that I—"

"That's what I mean. Believe me, I understand that the early days of building a business are crazy. My schedule is always packed, too. But it's good to pause and have fun sometimes. Right, Badger? Help me convince her to hang out with us for a while tonight."

He glanced up, his gaze warm. "We'd be honored to have you, Caitlin."

She hesitated. She hadn't gone dancing at the GG in forever. Badger and Hayley would knock themselves out making sure she had fun. She'd be living in this town with Aaron for a long time. Might as well start as she meant to go on. "Thank you. I'd love to stay."

Badger smiled. "Good call."

Evidently it was, because when she walked into the GG ten minutes later, Hayley was there to greet her, arms outstretched. "Badger texted me." She gave her a fierce hug. "Full steam ahead, girlfriend."

"I almost hid in my apartment, instead."

"And I wouldn't have blamed you. But I'm glad you didn't. We'll have a great time. Can I get you a beer?"

"Not until I'm off the clock, but after my thirty minutes are up, I'd love one."

"Just come to our table."

"Will do."

"One more thing." Arm around her shoulders, Hayley drew her aside and lowered her voice. "Ryker and April are at our table, so we'll have to watch what we say."

"Understood."

"Sheila may still be there when you show up, too, but she plans to eat, claim her one dance from Aaron and go get some sleep. She's had a rough trip."

"So I heard." She'd be fine if Sheila danced with Aaron. No problemo.

"I've told her Aaron isn't a good bet."

"You did? Why say that? He seems to like her." She congratulated herself for being evolved.

"Sheila likes him, too, but she was getting mixed signals. He was trying to be polite but his attention was on you the whole time."

"Oh." Her sudden urge to grin was not a good sign. She cleared her throat. "Tough luck for him. He screwed the pooch."

Hayley laughed. "He did, didn't he? Where'd you hear that expression?"

"*The Right Stuff*. It's a flyboy thing."

"That must be why Badger says it, then."

Caitlin gazed at her friend and sighed. "Why do pilots have to be so sexy?"

"Maybe you can't get into flight school unless you're hot. And speaking of hot, my groom has arrived. With my mom."

Caitlin turned toward the door. At the same moment, Warren left his seat at the bar, met his wife as she came in with Badger, and led her immediately toward the dance floor.

"Your dad has style."

"I agree."

"I need a video of them two-stepping." She dug both cameras out of her bag, held one and looped the other around her neck.

"Want me to take your bag to our table for safekeeping?"

"That would be great."

Hayley smiled at Badger as he approached. "Hey, bridegroom. Wanna join my folks on the dance floor?"

"You know it, darlin'."

"Be a sweetheart and run Caitlin's camera bag over to the table first, please." She winked at Caitlin.

"*Yes, ma'am.*" He took the bag, clearly eager to please. "Anythin' else I can do for you two lovely ladies?"

"Just one quick question." Caitlin tried to sound casual. Likely failed. "Will Aaron be at your table tonight?"

"He doesn't have to be. I can tell him to sit somewhere—"

"No, don't do that. I appreciate your gallantry, but this is the new normal. I'll deal."

_17_

Aaron put effort into dancing with Sheila. She was a nice woman and he wanted her to have a good time. She'd stopped flirting with him and judging from her comments, she'd figured out that he was interested in Caitlin.

At the end of it, she gave him a hug. "Thanks. Your photographer is a lucky lady."

"Not so sure about that." To begin with, Caitlin certainly wasn't his, and she might argue about the lucky part since he'd recently bamboozled her.

Sheila patted his chest. "Well, I am sure. And you're an excellent dancer. Maybe you'll gift me with one more turn around the floor tomorrow night."

"Let's plan on it." He escorted her to the table and Hayley left temporarily to take her back to the house.

Ryker stood and offered his hand to April. "Raven's set the bar pretty high just now, but I'm confident we can—"

"Ryker." April gazed at him.
"What?"

"We've talked about this. Not everything has to be a competition. I doubt anyone's keeping score."

Aaron caught Badger's eye and then they both ducked their heads to hide their grins. Ryker was the most competitive man in Eagles Nest. Probably in the entire state of Montana.

"Oh." Ryker rubbed the back of his neck. "You want to dance just for the hell of it?"

"Yes. Yes, I do."

He shrugged. "Okay."

"Thank you."

After they'd left the table, Badger just about killed himself laughing and Badger's laughter was more contagious than the common cold. Soon Aaron was wiping tears from his eyes and gasping for air.

Badger coughed a few times, took a breath and leaned back in his chair. "Do you suppose she knows that he's just goin' along with her to make life easier? He hasn't changed his attitude about competition one iota."

"She's a smart lady, so I think she knows." Aaron sipped his beer. "My guess is she's playing the long game. If she keeps at it, eventually he'll come around."

"Not Cowboy. He has a warrior's heart."

"Yeah, he does." Aaron glanced at his phone. "Seven minutes to go."

"Not that you're keeping track or anything."

"I just don't like the odds. Once Caitlin arrives at our table, four of us will be in possession of info we want to keep from the other two. That's an imbalance, and Nature abhors an imbalance."

"No, Nature abhors a vacuum."

"I'll bet Nature abhors an imbalance, too. It's the same principle. I should probably leave."

"You've been sayin' that ever since findin' out she'd be joinin' us. I notice you're still here."

"I had to stay long enough to dance with Sheila."

"I don't see you dancin' with Sheila at the moment. Matter of fact, I don't even see Sheila."

"Smartass."

"Face it, good buddy. You can't bear to leave when there's a chance you can make some headway if you hang around."

"Pathetic, isn't it?"

"I think it's kinda cute."

Aaron sent him a withering look. "That's because your gonads aren't the ones caught in the door."

"I thought it was your foot."

"It's all connected. If one thing's caught, the rest is, too."

"So here's what you're goin' to do. You're goin' to ask her to dance."

"She'll refuse."

"She won't if you ask her when April and Cowboy are sittin' here."

"That's not fair. She'll hate having to say yes. She'll hate dancing with me."

"If she does, then you don't have to push it and ask her again and you're no worse off than before. But I have five bucks that says she won't hate it."

"I'm not betting you. I can't take a bet I know I'll win."

"Suit yourself. Are you goin' to ask her?"

He nudged his hat back. "You really think she won't hate it?"

"She might at first."

"See? Now you're hedging."

"Well, she might because she knows you out-maneuvered her by askin' in front of Cowboy and April. But once you're on the dance floor you'll have body contact and she's susceptible to you in that regard."

"Maybe before, but she won't welcome it now."

"There's a chance she might, given a few bars of the dance number. You were canoodlin' with her on the dinin' table on Tuesday night. And doin' somethin' even more interestin' on Wednesday night. This is only Friday. Those memories are still fresh."

"Not as fresh as Thursday night's nightmare, when she was expecting Raven and Aaron Donahue showed up."

"Yeah, but Raven's the one she was gettin' friendly with Tuesday and Wednesday. When you're hip-to-hip, that'll remind her of the fun she had with that guy. It could be the first step in blendin' one identity with the other."

"Is that even possible?"

"Got to test it to find out."

He looked at the time on his phone. "Less than four minutes."

"You do realize she might not be exactly on your timetable. She—"

"Well, she's not. She's on her way here right now."

"Good thing you talked to her earlier. Took the edge off."

"In theory." In practice, he might as well be in the middle of a high-altitude test flight. Badger had offered him a sliver of hope with the dancing plan. So like Badger to figure these things out. She would agree to dance with him if he timed the request correctly.

The potential inherent in Badger's suggestion made him hyperventilate as she drew closer to the table. Lack of oxygen to the brain was never a good thing, especially when so much was at stake.

She approached warily. "Hey, guys."

"Hey, Caitlin!" Aaron winced as he and Badger spoke in tandem and leaped up together to pull out a chair for her. Badger drew back and let him handle the chair thing, but still. Comedy Central.

She glanced up at him as he scooted her in. "Thanks."

"What would you like to drink?"

She surveyed the bottles of McGavin's Pale Ale on the table. "A glass of red wine, please."

Maybe that order wasn't a statement. Maybe she was just in the mood for wine instead of McGavin's Pale Ale. But he wouldn't bet on it.

"I just signaled Ellen," Badger said. "She should come by shortly."

Caitlin grabbed her camera bag from the chair next to her and began tucking stuff away. "I may be getting paranoid, but I can't help thinking you two were over here plotting a strategy before I showed up."

"We were."

Her head jerked up and Badger gave her a big smile.

Aaron stared at him in shock. "Why would you say a thing like that?"

"Because she deserves to hear the truth after what we put her through."

"Damn straight." She hung her bag from the back of her chair and leaned forward, arms on the table. "What's your strategy?"

Aaron's jaw dropped as Badger outlined the dancing plan, even touching lightly on the idea that dancing could be a way to meld Raven and Aaron into one person.

"Wow, that's brilliant." She settled back in her chair and studied them, her unreadable gaze moving from Badger over to him. "Thanks for the heads up."

He had no words. Badger was always full of surprises, but this one would go down in the history books.

She continued to stare at him. "I could fake an injury."

He swallowed. "Yes, ma'am, you certainly could."

"But then I'd have to limp around for the rest of the night and that doesn't sound like much fun."

"No, ma'am."

"April and Ryker are on their way back," Badger said. "Time to switch topics."

"You bet." Caitlin turned toward Badger. "What did you think of the rehearsal?"

"Awesome. Loved every minute."

"Went better than I expected," Ryker chimed in. He helped April into her chair and settled into his. "Of course, Delilah didn't have the rings, so that lowered my stress level considerably."

And Aaron's was rising fast. Once the music started, he'd be up to bat. He hadn't been this nervous about asking a girl to dance since middle school.

"Relax, Cowboy." Badger picked up his beer. "Those rings will be fine."

The band should be playing by now. Why not? Aaron shifted restlessly in his chair.

"Delilah still stinks," Ryker said. "When she pranced up to the altar and wagged her tail, I caught a whiff of *eau de skunk*."

April patted his arm. "That'll be gone by tomorrow. Abigail and Luke are on it." She glanced toward the front door. "And here comes Hayley!"

Badger tapped a brief message on his phone before shoving back his chair. "If y'all will excuse me, I need to discuss somethin' with my bride."

You mean fill her in on the plan.

"Hayley and I will take another Pale Ale, if y'all wouldn't mind ordering for us when Ellen gets here."

Ryker nodded. "Got it."

"Thank you kindly. Appreciate it." He left quickly, intercepting Hayley before she made it to their table.

Ellen arrived moments later, took their drink order and hurried back to the bar.

Still not a peep from the band. The suspense was killing him.

"I am *so* glad Sheila got here in time for the rehearsal and dinner," April smiled at Aaron. "That was sweet of you to dance with her."

"I was happy to. She loves it and doesn't get much opportunity back home." He glanced toward the bandstand. Nicole and Bryce had left their table and were conferring with the musicians, for some reason. Somebody brought out Bryce's guitar.

Badger led Hayley back to the table and his gaze flicked to the bandstand. "Excellent."

"What are they doing up there?" Ryker frowned. "I thought Bryce and Nicole had the night off."

"They do. I just made a small request the other day and they agreed to indulge me."

Hayley gazed at him. "What are you up to, now?"

"Well, after all that debatin' about what we'd have them play for our first dance tomorrow night, I started thinkin' that our alternate choice should have its moment tonight."

"Aww, Badger!" She leaned over, put her arms around him and kissed him soundly on the mouth.

He smiled at her. "Hope you like it, darlin'. Usually Nicole does this as a solo, but they thought it would be more appropriate as a duet."

"I'm sure I'll love it."

A romantic song meant for Badger and Hayley would likely be a solo dance for them, if they even danced at all. Maybe everyone would just sit and listen. Taking a deep breath, Aaron leaned back in his chair.

Nicole stepped to the mic. "We've had a request from Badger to sing one of Hayley's favorite numbers. One of mine and Bryce's, too, as it happens."

Hayley wiped her eyes. "I'm tearing up."

"Good." Badger wrapped an arm around her shoulders and squeezed.

"Badger's also requested that the dancers out there come up and fill the floor. It'll be close quarters, but we're all family, right?" She spread her arms and the group yelled *right* in unison.

Aaron glanced at Caitlin. Her cheeks were pink and her breathing unsteady. He leaned closer. "Think you know what song they're talking about?"

She nodded but didn't look at him. "We talked about it once. She loves it, too."

His breath caught. Not such a coincidence, really. It was a popular song. But if that was the one coming up, this dance would be loaded with more significance than he'd planned on. Maybe it would turn out to be a different tune.

Nope. As Bryce lifted his guitar strap over his head and joined Nicole at the mic, he played the first few notes of *Breathe*.

_18_

Caitlin left her chair when Aaron stood and held out his hand. Placing her hand in his, she met his gaze as the first tender lyrics of the song floated around them. She'd danced to this song in Raven's strong arms. But the intensity in Aaron's golden eyes sent a clear message. He would be the one holding her tonight.

He gave her a soft smile, turned and led her to the dance floor. Miraculously he found an opening in the swirling mass of dancers and drew her close as the current swept them into the midst of organized chaos.

Creating distance between his body and hers wasn't an option. The crush of the other couples kept them locked together.

Instead of making the steps more difficult, the forced proximity kept her focused on every sensuous point of contact. His muscles flexed and hers responded with intuitive grace.

His chest brushed hers in rhythm with the music. Their hips swiveled in perfect alignment. Dancing as foreplay. If they'd been naked, they would be making love.

As the tension built to a fever pitch, she resisted the urge to look up, to complete the intimate connection. Raven's shadowed eyes had been part of the fantasy. Aaron's direct gaze was all too real.

Caught in this whirlpool of sensation, she chose the safety of staring at the collar of his black shirt and the tanned skin revealed by two pearl snaps he'd left undone.

Maybe not so safe. His strong neck and firm jaw radiated masculinity. A drop of sweat slid into the hollow of his throat where his pulse beat. She could hear him breathing.

The scent of him—shaving lotion, soap, shampoo and musk—taunted her with images of an open shirt, a muscled chest sprinkled with dark hair, a rendezvous in the dark, skin to skin...hot kisses, pleasure...

Urges beyond her control dragged her gaze upward, sliding over his strong chin to his talented mouth. He'd kissed her with reckless abandon, as if he'd been impatiently waiting for her and couldn't contain his joy.

No man had ever kissed her that way. His urgency had fueled hers. But when he'd laced desire with tenderness, conveying without words that she was cherished...the walls had come down.

If she could experience that again...but what if it had been an illusion? What if the cloaked atmosphere and the shared secret had skewed her perception?

He pulled her in tight and spun her one more time. All outward movement stopped, but her heart raced on and her world continued to whirl. The music faded away as the other dancers clapped and cheered. She struggled for breath.

"That's all." His breathing was ragged, too. "Song's over." Yet he hadn't let her go. "Having you in my arms again is…incredible."

She gathered her courage and gazed into his eyes. The heat blazing there made her gulp. "I thought…I could handle this. But it's not as easy as I expected."

"This?"

"The situation. You. Whoever you are."

The pleasure faded from his expression. "Guess it's not as simple as Badger seems to think."

"Not even close. I'm attracted to you, or at least to the side of you I spent time with this week." She sucked in another lungful of air. "But you're also the guy who pretended to be someone else to trick me into liking you."

He slowly released her. "It seemed like my only choice."

"That doesn't make it right. I'm still dealing with the implications. The issue of trust."

Pain flashed in his eyes. "I'm not an untrustworthy man."

"And yet—"

"Look, you just admitted that something special happens when we're together. If I hadn't pretended to be someone else, we wouldn't have found that out."

"The band's playing again. We should—"

"Okay." He looped an arm around her shoulders and guided her to a secluded spot away from the dance floor and beyond the polished antique bar.

His touch was her kryptonite. She eased away from the protective curve of his arm and faced him. "So the end justifies the means?"

"Maybe." He ran his fingers through his hair. "Last night I told Badger that I didn't regret anything." He held her gaze. "Boil my privates in oil if you want, but I'd do it all again."

"Even knowing that I'd be furious with you?"

He gazed at her. "Furious is better than indifferent."

"I wasn't indifferent to you. I just—"

"Would never have considered spending time with me. Well, now you have. You've confirmed my hunch that we'd be great together. I know what I'd like to do with that information, but I can't speak for you."

"Of course you'd be ready to start a relationship with me. I've been the same person all along. But you're this split personality and I can't—"

"So Raven and Aaron are still two separate entities to you?"

"*Yes*. I know Badger was hoping that a dance would fix that, but like I said, it's not that simple."

"Then how about a few more dances to solidify the concept?"

"And then what?"

"Well...not that we'd have to, but we could maybe test out a more private setting."

Her jaw tightened. "And have sex?"

"Or, as I prefer to say, make love."

"Tonight? Seems a little nervy on your part."

"Is it really such a stretch? We almost did on Tuesday night. We likely would have if you hadn't knocked over my books."

"*Your books*." She stared at him. "I forgot all about that."

He smiled. "Want to get together and geek out over Dick Francis?"

Just when she'd worked herself into a state of indignation, he had to say something adorable. "So it's either have sex or talk about our favorite author?"

He shrugged. "Or both. I'd be hard-pressed to choose one over the other."

"Liar."

"Yeah, I'd rather talk about Dick Francis."

"Sure you would." Now he was being playful, like Raven. Way too appealing. "I'm really sorry about the dent in the dust cover."

"I'm not. I'll think of you every time I notice it."

"See? You'll notice it because it's a new dent. I damaged one of your rare books."

"You don't get all the credit. I should've seen that stack sitting there."

"But I put them—"

"I'm glad we knocked them over. We were headed for disaster that night."

"Oh?"

"As Badger explained the next day, once we stepped into that hall, we would have crossed the line from Raven's World into Aaron Donahue Land."

"I don't get it."

"My second bedroom is an office. If you'd figured that out—"

"Ah. The game would have been over. Then why did you let it go that far?"

He glanced down and sighed. When he looked up again, regret shone in his eyes. "My brain took a little vacay. Not proud of admitting it."

"So that's why we went parking Wednesday night?"

"Yep. Full disclosure. I almost rented a bedroom set for that office. Could've had everything arranged before you got there."

Fascinating. "Why didn't you?"

"My conscience kicked in. Taking you to bed would've been wrong."

"I wouldn't say that, exactly. Precipitous, maybe, but we're consenting adults. I wouldn't label it—"

"You didn't know who I was."

"That didn't stop you from kissing me."

"You kissed me first."

So she had. Discussing it was having a predictable effect on her libido. "Since I clearly wanted you, why draw the line at taking me to bed?"

"It was the compromise I made with myself. Kissing was okay, giving you pleasure was okay. Allowing myself pleasure would mean I was taking advantage of the situation. Of you."

His reasoning made a kind of convoluted sense. It was gallant in a way. "And here I wondered if you had some terrible scar, or a sexual hang-up that kept you from having normal—"

"I told you I didn't."

"I know, which made it even more puzzling. I came over Thursday night determined to find out what was keeping you—and me, for that matter—from enjoying ourselves in your bed."

"Nothing, now."

She gazed at him. "Nothing and everything."

"Meaning?"

"I take it you'd like to pick up where we left off Wednesday night."

"The answer is yes, but I have a strong suspicion that's not the right answer."

"I wasn't planning to stay after I took pictures here. Virginia talked me into it."

"So I heard. And Badger offered to relocate me to another table so you'd be more comfortable. When you told him that wasn't necessary, I hoped that you—"

"I wanted to find out whether you and I could function as casual friends because that's all I intended for us to be. Ever."

"Ouch."

"Then you and Badger came up with this dance plan. I give him credit for laying it out in advance."

"Me, too. It was the right move."

"Catching me by surprise wouldn't have gone well for you."

"Probably not." He sighed. "I'm just so damned sure we could make a go of it that I'm willing to do whatever it takes to influence your thinking."

"Whatever it takes?"

"Except for one thing. I won't legally change my name."

"I would never expect you to do that."

"That's good, because I won't. My mother gave it to me and although I never knew my dad, she says he was a great guy, so I'm proud of my last name, too."

"What's your middle name?"

He smiled. "Henry."

"So would you consider—"

"No. Sorry. Not even for you, and it would be only a partial fix, anyway. I'd still have the Donahue part."

"I agree it's a lame solution."

"But it sounds like you might be looking for a better one."

"There's an obvious answer to this."

"If you mean using Raven, maybe, although that's more of a buddy thing with Badger and Cowboy. I'm Aaron to everyone else, so I don't think that's—"

"I wasn't going to suggest Raven, either. The obvious fix is for you to find a woman without an aversion to your name."

He was silent for a few moments. "Is that what you want me to do?"

"Well, I—"

"Let me put it another way. If nothing that happened this week has changed your mind about spending time with a guy named Aaron Donahue..." He swallowed. "I'll give up."

"And if I tell you that that's the case, you'll abandon all thoughts of me and turn your attention to someone else?"

"There's no way I can abandon all thoughts of you. You're embedded in my brain, likely will be for some time. But I won't be pestering you anymore."

Her heart thumped painfully. She should say it. Put them both out of their misery. No more games. No more angst. No more kisses...

"I'm encouraged that you didn't just blurt it out. Have I made some inroads, after all?"

"Why can't your name be John Smith?"

"Because it's not. And never will be. That's the bottom line. If you're going to hate my name for the rest of your life, then we need to call it."

"Would it be terrible if I asked for a little time to think about it?"

"Not at all. Take whatever you need."

"Twenty-four hours. I don't want to leave you hanging."

"Why not? Wouldn't that be a fitting revenge?"

"I'm losing my taste for revenge. Twenty-four hours is enough time."

"And I get a short reprieve. I'd rather not hear the bad news now. This way I can enjoy the wedding while telling myself there's still a chance you'll give me a try."

"Hmm."

He held her gaze as the band launched into their next number. "That's a waltz. Want to take a few turns around the floor for old times' sake?"

She smiled. "I'll think better if I'm at home instead of waltzing with you."

"That's what I'm afraid of. Since I have twenty-four hours, I'm not above using them to my advantage."

"I can't stop you from attempting that, so I'm heading home."

"Can I kiss you goodbye?"

"No, I'm afraid not. I don't think at all when you're kissing me."

"Curses." He gave her a lopsided smile. "Foiled again."

__19__

After Caitlin picked up her camera gear and left the table to say goodbye to the other members of the wedding party, Ryker glanced at Aaron. "Something going on between you two?"

"We're just friends."

He nodded. "Okay. Thought I was picking up on something, but my mistake. Just wondered because, you know...the name thing."

"It's a problem."

"Too bad."

"Yep." He didn't look at Badger. When Ryker finally heard the story, which he would eventually, the ca-ca would hit the fan.

He waited until Ryker and April returned to the dance floor before he told Badger and Hayley about the latest development.

Badger nudged back his hat. "I'd call that progress."

"She could shoot me down tomorrow night."

Hayley leaned over and gave his arm a squeeze. "Such a ridiculous problem, Aaron."

"Not so ridiculous," Badger said. "I get a case of the hives lookin' at our marriage license. I hate seein' Thaddeus Livingston printed there instead of Badger."

"If that's supposed to make me feel better," Aaron said, "it doesn't."

"It's supposed to illustrate the depth of the problem. On the other hand, the fact that Caitlin's takin' time to think about this is very encouragin'."

"Aside from the name issue, she likes you," Hayley said. "I could tell that when I looked at the pictures."

Aaron's eyebrows lifted. "She showed them to you?"

"Last night."

"Why?"

"She was feeling a little foolish because she didn't recognize you right away. She thought the pictures would help explain why she got distracted by the fantasy. Have you seen them?"

"No, and now I'm curious."

"Me, too." Badger grinned at him. "Never thought of you as pin-up material."

Aaron rolled his eyes. "I was just standing on the sidewalk."

"Flexing your muscles for the camera?"

"*No*. Sheesh."

"He was wearing his flight jacket and his aviators," Hayley said. "Looking very *Top Gun*-ish."

Badger groaned. "I can guaran-damn-tee that wasn't on purpose."

"It sure as hell wasn't."

"Whether it was intentional or not, that's what Caitlin saw, and she's susceptible to flyboys."

"See?" Badger pointed a finger at him. "Told you that was goin' to help your cause."

"Yeah, but that's when the flyboy was Raven."

"You should take her up in the Cessna. Hayley loves it when I take her flyin'. It does wonders for my image."

"He's not kidding. It's his favorite way to get on my good side when we have a fight. It's hard to stay mad at a guy when he's demonstrating his skills at fifteen thousand feet."

"I hope you're referring to his piloting skills."

Badger wiggled his eyebrows. "Wouldn't you like to know?"

"No, I would not. Oh, and FYI, Luke and Wes are headed this way."

"Does Luke still have that *I just won the lottery* expression on his face?"

"Yep. Just like you. But I think he's had more beer than you. He's weaving a bit."

"Hey, Aaron!" Luke came around the table and plopped into the chair Caitlin had vacated. "Did we set a time to be at your house in the morning?"

Wes, Luke's best man, took Ryker's chair, turned it backwards and straddled it. "I told him it was eleven, but he insists he needs to hear it from you."

Aaron gave his attention to Luke, whose smile was slightly off-center. "You're due at my house at eleven. Ryker's bringing our clothes."

"Our tux-ee-does?"

"Exactly. I bought eggs and bacon. You guys were going to bring goodies from Pie in the Sky."

Wes nodded. "Ingrid will have that packed up and ready to go first thing."

"Abby won't be baking tomorrow." Luke's gaze became dreamy and unfocused. "She'll be having her hair done and her fingernails done and her toenails done. I told her *Abby, you're already beautiful! You don't need any of that!*" He swept his arms out, almost smacking Aaron in the face. "Can you believe it? Tomorrow I'm getting *married!*"

Aaron patted him on the back. "So I heard."

"Badger and me, we're getting *married*! Right, Badger?"

"Right, Luke." Badger grinned. "And what a darlin' couple we'll make."

"Hey! I'm not marrying *you*. I'm marrying Abby. And you're marrying Hayley. You need to get that straight, Badger. It's important."

"Yes, sir." Badger gave Hayley a fond glance. "It surely is."

Wes stood. "Luke, are we good then? Got the deets you needed?"

Luke gave a nod and used the table to push himself upright. "We're good. Let's go see Abby. I miss her. Miss her like the devil."

After they left, Hayley smiled. "I don't think I've ever seen Luke smashed."

"Doesn't happen often," Badger said. "Kinda touchin' to see him let go like this. He adores that woman. Tomorrow's a big day for him."

"For me, too, sweetie."

Badger reached for her hand and clasped it between both of his as he gazed into her eyes. "For me, too, darlin'."

Aaron glanced down. Some moments between couples weren't meant to be shared, even with good friends. He pushed back his chair. "Guess I'll be shoving off."

Hayley looked his way. "Aw, Aaron, don't feel you have to. I promise we're not going into permanent lovebird mode."

"I'm promisin' no such thing, darlin'. I love this guy like a brother, but I spent most of last night with him. You and me have some catchin' up to do."

"I'm sure." Aaron stood. "Besides, if I'm hosting tomorrow, I need to straighten up the house. Badger, I'll see you at eleven. Hayley, I'll see you at the altar."

"Yeah." She gazed up at him. "Can you believe the big day is almost here?"

"Pretty incredible." Badger's wedding day was always going to be significant. But now—one way or another—tomorrow would change his life.

***

At eleven the next morning, pickups lined his street and his living room had become party central. Badger and Luke had commandeered the kitchen and were frying up eggs and bacon. Luke had brought Delilah, who was successfully coaxing Badger to feed her bacon.

Ryker had brought in a clothes rack for the Western-styled tuxedos. Wes came through the front door with two large, fragrant boxes of pastries from Pie in the Sky. Wes's brother Gage, Luke's other groomsman, arrived with pre-mixed Bloody Marys in two large jugs.

"Anybody who spills that drink on the tuxes will answer to me," Ryker announced.

"No worries," Badger called from the kitchen. "I won't be wearin' my tux when I'm enjoyin' Bloody Marys. Matter of fact, I'll be naked."

"Just don't go out on the porch in that condition," Aaron said.

"Never fear. Wouldn't want to be causin' a riot among the fine ladies in your neighborhood."

Ryker groaned. "Here it comes."

"If I do any porch sittin'," Badger continued as if Ryker hadn't spoken. "I'll take care to cover my impressive manhood with a generously sized towel."

"A washcloth should do it," Luke said.

Ryker laughed. "Forget the washcloth. A hot pad's plenty big enough."

"I brought some of those little paper coasters from the GG," Gage said as he poured Bloody Marys into beer cups. "He can have one of those."

"Notice that I'm choosin' not to respond to your insecure ravin', which proves that I am, in fact, possessed of the most amazin'—"

"Ego of all," Luke said. "Eggs are ready. Do you have bacon over there, Mister Well-Hung, or have you fed it all to the dog?"

"I have bacon, and it's cooked to a delicate crispiness that'll have you all salivatin' and singin' my praises."

"Hallelujah!" Aaron called out. "Bring it on in here!" He'd pulled the dining table away from the corner and added the extra leaf.

By using his office chair and a folding chair he kept in a back closet, he had seating for six. His first real party, unless he counted having Caitlin over. He counted it.

The men set upon the food as if they hadn't eaten a meal in a week. Bloody Mary cups were refilled. Despite his boast, Badger kept his clothes on.

The gathering grew louder and more bawdy—much like Aaron's squadron buddies had behaved on leave. Shouldn't need a wedding to create a fun occasion like this. He'd do it more often.

Badger paused in the middle of telling a joke and pulled his phone out of his pocket. "Excuse me, y'all. My phone's vibratin'." He read the text and glanced up. "Aaron, Caitlin's been tryin' to get in touch. Check your phone."

He took it out of his pocket. He'd silenced it. Hadn't expected a call or a text from anybody. Especially her.

Had she made up her mind already? If she'd decided that quickly, chances were good it wouldn't be the verdict he was hoping for. He took a quick breath and tapped on the screen.

Miscommunication. Turns out Virginia not only expected me to take pictures of the bridal party's preparations, she also assumed I'd drive over there and get a few of the men getting ready. Can you accommodate that? Let me know.

He let out a breath. Just some wedding stuff. Of course, it meant he'd see her soon instead of at the ceremony later today. That was okay.

Everybody was laughing and making comments about Badger's joke. Aaron banged on his plate to get their attention. "Caitlin needs to come over and take some shots of us getting ready. How do you—"

"Getting ready?" Luke frowned. "That sounds like a dicey idea."

"Yeah," Wes said. "I'm not crazy about a wedding album picture of me stepping into my pants."

"I wouldn't mind," Badger said.

"We've established you're willing to flash the world," Ryker said. "We need more info, Raven."

"I'll ask her." He typed a quick message. *Nobody wants a picture of them putting on their pants. Except Badger. He doesn't care.*

She came back with a smiley face. *No risqué shots. I won't come in until you're all decent.*

That's never gonna happen with this crowd.

This time the emoji was laughing. *Just text me when I can come in without blushing.*

Will do. I'll estimate about three this afternoon would be good.

Thx.

Welcome. He tucked his phone away. "She doesn't want anybody flashing her. I told her to come around three. So have your pants on by three."

Badger gazed at him, eyebrows raised. "Interestin' development. Her comin' here."

"Mm." He glanced at the table, littered with the remains of their breakfast. Having her in his house again under totally different circumstances would be weird. But any chance to be with her was a bonus he'd gladly accept.

_20_

Arriving at Aaron's house at three in the afternoon with a party going on inside destroyed any chance of Caitlin experiencing déjà vu. For one thing, she couldn't park where she usually did.

She slowed. Badger's truck was in the primo spot right in front. She counted three others lined up on this side of the street, plus Wild Creek's big white van.

The other side of the street wasn't much better. Someone else on this block must be having people over. She'd passed one open spot on the other side. Looked like she'd have to turn around.

Wait. Was Badger about to move his vehicle? Sure enough, the truck pulled out and headed down the block. He made a U-turn at the end of the street and came back toward her.

When he was directly opposite her Jeep, he braked and slid the tinted window down. Not Badger. Aaron.

She lowered her window. "What's going on?"

He flashed her a smile. "I'm moving his truck so you can park in your usual spot." He was wearing his aviators, a white tux shirt open at the neck and a tight-fitting gray vest.

She had to guess at the rest of the outfit, but the top half was primo. He wore it well. "That's sweet of you, but—"

"I'm a sweet guy. Go ahead and pull in. I'll park this baby and be right back."

"Thanks."

"You bet." He raised the window and drove away.

She took a deep breath. He'd said he'd use these twenty-four hours to further his cause. He'd made a good start. Gallantry never went out of style.

By the time she'd sandwiched her Jeep between a pickup and the Wild Creek van, Aaron was in her rearview mirror, striding down the middle of the residential street like Gary Cooper in High Noon.

The tux pants matched the vest and wow, did he do them justice. She wouldn't mind having a video of him coming toward her. She reached for the zipper on her camera bag. But...maybe not the right move. Yeah, definitely not. She kept the bag closed.

Grabbing the bag from the passenger seat, she climbed out of her Jeep. "That outfit's gorgeous." Mostly because he was wearing it.

"Thanks. Not my doing. Badger and Luke made the choice."

"They have good taste. Is everybody already dressed?"

"They all have their pants on. Beyond that, I make no promises. I got ready ahead of time so I could move Badger's truck."

"I appreciate the effort. Guess I'm spoiled. I got here and thought *oh, no, where will I park?* Fact is, I could have parked where you just did."

"Not when I'm around." He held her gaze. The sexy aviators screened his golden eyes, but clearly he was looking straight at her. "I would have done it, anyway, but I needed a reason to catch you before you came in."

"Is Ryker asking questions?"

"Last night he wanted to know if there was anything between us. I said we were just friends."

"I worried about that after I left last night. We were off in a corner talking for a long time."

"He's dropped the subject. But when you come in the house, we need to act like you've never been there."

"Oh, right!"

"Since Badger's in on this, he was all for my truck-moving plan."

"I'm glad you reminded me. I like to think I wouldn't have blown it, but I have a lot on my mind."

"I know." His chest heaved, straining the material of his vest. "Me, too."

"But speaking of Ryker, let's get in there before we give him another reason to wonder."

"Good idea. The clock's ticking. Less than two hours 'till show time."

"Tell me about it." She looped the strap of her camera bag over her shoulder and walked around the front of the Jeep. "I still need to change into my dress."

He followed her. "You're wearing a dress?"

"Shocking, isn't it?"

"I don't think I've ever seen you in one."

"Probably not." She started up the walk. "I hardly ever wear a dress, but weddings seem to call for it. I like blending in with the guests. The less I stand out, the more everyone will forget I'm there."

"Everyone but me. I'll—uh-oh, guess I didn't close the door tight enough. Someone's coming out to greet you."

Delilah shoved herself the rest of the way through the partially opened door, raced across the porch and bounded down the steps, wagging her tail and grinning.

"Delilah!" Caitlin dropped to one knee and wrapped her arms around the dog's furry neck. "I don't care what Ryker says. You smell fine to me."

Delilah wiggled, whined and licked her face.

"I didn't know you and Delilah were such buddies. I saw you taking her picture yesterday, but—"

"Oh, we're buddies. Aren't we, Delilah?" She scratched behind the dog's ears. "Luke and Abigail hired me to shoot some professional pictures of her and we got along great. Sometimes, if I'm lucky, Kendra is dog-sitting Delilah when I go riding. I get to take her along."

"Sounds like fun."

"Yep, it is." She stood. "Okay, girl, we have to get cracking. We have places to go and grooms to shoot." With one last pat, she started up the steps with Delilah at her heels.

Aaron laughed. "That line would fit in a Dick Francis novel."

She glanced over her shoulder and smiled. "So it would."

"Have you started any of the books?"

"Dipped into *Nerve* this morning." She paused by the door, which was still partly open. Male laughter spilled out, followed by Badger's Southern drawl and more laughter. A country tune played in the background. She stepped back.

"Something wrong?"

She lowered her voice. "I probably shouldn't just walk in as if I'm used to doing it. You'd better announce me and escort me inside."

"Will do." He stepped around her and opened the door wider. "Caitlin's here!" He ushered her into the house as the men called out cheerful greetings and leaped to their feet. That was the protocol in Eagles Nest.

"Hey, guys." Badger, Ryker and Wes had been sitting at the dining table with poker chips, cards, and beer cups likely filled with something alcoholic.

Luke and Gage had turned the easy chairs to face each other and had been playing checkers on the table where she and Raven—*Aaron*—had set their beer bottles. No fire in the fireplace.

At three in the afternoon, sunlight poured through the windows. The room wasn't the same at all, yet the lingering scent of wood smoke and those two comfy chairs brought it all back—the muted lighting, the dancing, the kissing...

Focus, Caitlin. "The gray pants look sharp. Like the shirts, too." They'd all buttoned their shirts, but only Ryker had bothered to tuck his in.

"Luke and I did good with these outfits." Badger came toward her. "You're lookin' prettier than a speckled pup."

"Thanks." She smiled. "I'll bet you say that to all the girls."

"He does," Luke said. "He needs a new charming Southern compliment because that one's growing moss."

"I can change it up." He cleared his throat. "Darlin', you're more beautiful than a pecan pie coolin' on a farmhouse windowsill."

"Thank you, Badger. You're more impressive than a Hasselblad."

He blinked. "Now there's a compliment to treasure."

Ryker looked over at him and grinned. "You have no idea what that is."

"I'm not sayin' yet. Waitin' to see if you know."

"I don't." Wes grabbed his phone and tapped on the screen. "It's a camera. Very expensive one."

"I knew that." Badger smoothed the front of his pleated shirt. "Is this the right look for my close-up? Or are we supposed to be pulled together and spit-shined for this photo shoot?"

"Virginia was vague about what kind of images she's after, so we'll have to wing it."

"I'm exceptional at wingin' it." He swept an arm around the room. "Here's your settin', Caitlin. Think it'll work?"

Nicely played, Badger. She took her time surveying the familiar room. "It's a good space, casual. And homey. How about this setup—all you guys at the table, hanging out, petting Delilah, playing poker and drinking...whatever it is you're drinking?"

"Water." Ryker spoke the word as a command, which it probably had been. "Once the clothes came out of the garment bags, the Bloody Mary jugs went back to Gage's truck."

"Water." She chuckled. "I guess it doesn't matter what's in those cups. They look like they should have booze in them. They fit the mood I'm going for—six manly guys playing a little poker, sipping adult beverages and savoring the calm before the storm."

Luke nodded. "I like it. I think Mom would, too."

"Badger?"

He nodded. "Excellent idea."

"After that I can film everybody getting ready for the big moment, when it's time to tuck in the shirts, put on the vests and grab the coats."

"The beginnin' of the adventure." Badger looked over at Luke. "I can't wait."

"Me, either."

"I want to get you two saying that on the video. Okay, everybody. Gather around the poker table."

"Luke and me got bumped out, though," Gage said. 'It's just the other four guys. That's why we were over there playing checkers."

"Nobody has to know that, either. For now, we'll create the illusion that you're all in the game, having a rousing good time."

"In other words, we're setting the scene." Aaron exchanged a glance with Badger.

He nodded. "Understood."

She just bet they understood. Those co-conspirators knew exactly how illusions worked. "Luke and Gage need to have poker chips at their places, though."

"Used nearly all of them," Aaron said.

"Could you redistribute what's on the table?"

Ryker frowned. "Redistribute the chips?"

He looked so pained that she swallowed a bubble of laughter. Quite likely the ginormous stack belonged to him. "I'm not a poker player, so maybe that's a bad idea, especially if there's money involved."

"There isn't," Ryker said. "This was a last-minute idea." He pulled out his phone and took a picture of the table. "Okay, redistribute." He grinned and held up his phone. "I have my evidence."

Badger clapped him on the shoulder. "Congratulations on abandonin' the field for the good of the order, Cowboy. April would be proud."

"Alrighty, gentlemen," Aaron sat down and flexed his fingers. "Help yourselves to Cowboy's stash and ante in." Picking up the deck, he began shuffling. "Five-card stud, jokers wild."

He flipped cards off the top of the stack with practiced ease, a riverboat gambler, complete with tight-fitting vest.

She wouldn't have thought she'd be attracted to that image at all, let alone wildly attracted. Wrong-o. Aaron taking command of the poker table was sexy as hell.

He picked up his cards and glanced at her. "Are you going to shoot video of this or stills?"

"Vid—" She paused to clear the hoarseness from her throat. "Video first."

"Need some water?"

"Good idea."

"There's a pitcher in the fridge."

"I know."

His eyes widened.

Whoops. "I mean, I assumed you had one. Everybody does, right?" She hurried into the kitchen and squeezed her eyes shut. Maybe nobody would notice that little slip.

_21_

After Caitlin left, Aaron waited for Cowboy to take him aside. The guy already had his suspicions. Then again, maybe nobody had noticed her rapt attention while he'd dealt the first hand. She'd looked at him like he was her favorite piece of candy in the box.

He'd wanted to shout for joy. Clearly she was into him, which meant this could turn out to be the best damned day of his life. But he hadn't wanted anybody else, least of all Cowboy, to start speculating. Time for damage control.

Except that startling her and offering a glass of water had made things worse. Nobody commented on Caitlin's flustered behavior, though, not during the final preparations at the house or the brief time the guys waited in a back room of the venue for their cue.

On the other hand, Cowboy had more important things to worry about than Aaron's love life. The double wedding ceremony had thrown him into military command mode, but he wasn't in total charge of the mission—a double whammy for a born leader.

He'd lost the battle of the rings. Despite his protests, Delilah would soon be in control of a small fortune in wedding jewelry. He'd talked Luke out of attaching the rings to her collar until they were inside the building, but she would still carry them down the aisle.

Cowboy was also tasked with getting Badger's valuable bagpipes to the chapel and stashing them somewhere up front in readiness for the promised concert. He'd transferred them from Badger's truck to the ranch van, and from the van to the chapel. Leaving them on the floor up near the altar hadn't worked for him, so he'd commandeered a metal folding chair to set them on.

Virginia had objected to his practical but inelegant solution. He'd negotiated a compromise by locating a drapery in a back room to throw over the metal chair. Yeah, Cowboy might not have the bandwidth to question Aaron's relationship with Caitlin. Just as well.

Luke attached the rings to Delilah's jeweled collar. In the chapel, Bryce and Nicole launched their playlist of gentle yet upbeat country love songs to welcome the guests.

On Cowboy's signal, Badger led their group of three to the right side of the altar and Luke led Wes and Gage to the left side. Each of them carried a white Stetson tucked in the crook of his arm the way men in vintage photos held their bowlers.

No minister stood at the altar ready to perform the double ceremony. Warren would end up there eventually, after he'd walked Hayley and

Abigail, one on each arm, down the aisle. Abigail would be part of a loving family again after losing her folks several years ago.

Aaron scanned the crowd for a glimpse of Caitlin. He looked past her twice before focusing more closely on a woman with lustrous curls and a gauzy, form-fitting dress in shades of green and blue.

The woman turned, aimed a camera in his direction briefly, and hurried to the other side of the room in a graceful blur of color. Caitlin.

"See someone special, Raven?" Cowboy's voice was soft but distinct.

Aaron continued to face forward and his lips barely moved. "What makes you think that?"

"You sucked in a breath. I know that sound. Usually means a guy's just been blindsided by a pretty woman."

He remained silent. He'd neither confirm nor deny.

"Caitlin told me there was no way you two would connect. Seems you've managed to find one."

"Jury's still out." His twenty-four-hour reprieve would be over soon and he'd get the verdict. Judging from the way she'd looked at him today, he had a fighting chance.

"I wish you luck, buddy."

"Thanks." He regretted leaving Cowboy out of the loop. Even if Badger had been right and their Air Force buddy would have disapproved, it didn't sit right that he'd been kept in the dark. But what was done was done. Now was not the time to correct the situation.

The remaining three McGavin brothers, their two cousins from Scotland and Michael Murphy kept busy ushering guests to their seats as the hour drew near. The renovated barn was spacious, yet it was packed, both with Eagles Nesters and folks from out of town.

Aaron located Caitlin again, this time crouched near the far wall, switching lenses. When she stood up and turned in his direction, her skirt swirled around her, shimmering in the lights. A dress made for dancing.

He hadn't asked if she was planning to take pictures all evening. Her promise to give him an answer sometime tonight had implied they'd have time to talk, maybe even share a dance.

The venue had two reception areas, one indoors and one open-air with heaters spaced among the tables for cool nights like this one. Both couples had voted for the outdoor facility with its canopy of twinkling white lights. He couldn't ask for a more romantic setting.

Bryce and Nicole finished their number and paused. The soft murmurs from the guests ceased. Caitlin slipped behind Gage, Wes and Luke to position herself where the minister would eventually stand. The opening chords of Shania Twain's *From This Moment On* filled the chapel as Delilah appeared at the far end of the aisle.

Everyone turned to look, snap pictures and smile. During the rehearsal, she'd come straight down the aisle. But that was yesterday. The pews had been mostly empty.

Delilah calmly surveyed the situation before setting out with a clear plan to take advantage of the vast potential for strokes and ear scratches. She stopped at each row, moving from side to side so she wouldn't miss a single opportunity to be petted, photographed and cooed over.

"Knew it," Cowboy muttered. "Knew she'd be a pain. This could take—" He paused as the dog's behavior changed.

Delilah's head came up and she faced the front of the chapel. Then she trotted briskly forward, tail wagging.

"She's comin' to me," Badger murmured.

"Or Luke," Cowboy said.

She ignored both men and headed for the position Warren would eventually occupy, the spot Caitlin had temporarily appropriated. The music nearly obscured the sounds of Caitlin quietly praising the dog and a cookie crunching.

"Remind me to thank her," Cowboy murmured.

"I will."

As Nicole and Bryce continued to sing *From This Moment On,* April in vibrant yellow and Roxanne in fuchsia appeared at the far end of the aisle, each carrying a colorful bouquet. Walking side-by-side with measured steps in time to the music, they approached the altar and the men standing there.

Cowboy's sharp intake of breath made Aaron smile. The imposing soldier had been bushwhacked by April in a flowing gown with flowers in her hair. She took her place next to Aaron.

Next came Sheila in turquoise and Ingrid in deep green. Ingrid focused her gaze and her happy smile on Wes. Sheila's glance held his and she gave him a friendly wink before taking her place next to Ryker.

Nicole and Bryce brought the Shania Twain song to a close and let silence reign for a few seconds, allowing the suspense to build. The number Abigail and Hayley had chosen for their entrance with Warren was a closely guarded secret.

When Nicole and Bryce dove into the happy beat of Taylor Swift's *Love Story*, the guests stood and turned. Anticipation was thick in the air. Abigail, Hayley and Warren didn't disappoint. They came out dancing.

Not just a little step here and there, either. When they opened with a complicated line dance, Aaron figured they'd spent hours choreographing and practicing this sucker. With fake bouquets, too, because both women included their bridal bouquets as part of the routine. He glanced back at Caitlin, who'd positioned herself perfectly to video the action. No doubt she'd been in on this.

The guests greeted the line dance with laughter and applause. As everyone clapped in rhythm with the song, a grinning Badger donned his white hat so he could clap along with everyone else. All the guys followed his lead.

Warren segued into a three-way maneuver, expertly twirling each bride in turn. Hayley and Abigail partnering for a quick two-step and Warren demonstrated some hilarious hip-hop skills that brought whistles of admiration. All three shimmied the last few feet before throwing up their hands and giving each other high fives.

The guests roared their approval. Aaron cheered until his throat was sore. Tradition went out the window as Badger swept Hayley up and whirled her around while Luke busted some moves with Abigail. Mopping his brow with a handkerchief and polishing his glasses, Warren smiled at Virginia, who applauded wildly from the front row. She gave him two thumbs up and blew him several kisses.

Amidst the commotion, Aaron caught movement in his peripheral vision. Caitlin was taking advantage of the hubbub to unobtrusively change her vantage point. She hurried down the side aisle and around the back of the last pew to stop partway up the middle aisle and crouch there, camera at the ready.

As everyone settled into their seats, Warren stepped forward. "Dear friends, we're gathered here to unite not one, but two couples in matrimony. Because I'm not qualified to choose who shall be married first, we'll let God decide. I'll flip a coin."

He got a laugh for that.

"Heads it'll be Hayley and Badger, tails, Abigail and Luke." Pulling a quarter out of his pocket, he flipped it in the air and leaned down to peer at the coin on the floor. "Tails! Abigail and Luke, come on down."

Aaron chuckled. "I love this guy."

"Me, too," April said. "He's being funny now, but he gets solemn when he starts the actual ceremony."

Ryker nodded. "He helped us write our own vows."

"Didn't know that." Aaron edged a little closer so he wouldn't miss parts of it like he had with Ryker's. The setting in a meadow with twittering birds and everyone on horseback had made hearing difficult.

This ceremony certainly meant a lot to Luke and Abigail. Their words to each other were tender and they choked up a little as they said them. Warren did, too. A few people in the audience sniffled. Virginia watched with tears streaming down her cheeks.

Aaron's chest grew tight with longing. A vague restlessness he'd dealt with for years was transforming into something approaching a goal. The vision wasn't clear yet, but he had a hunch it had quite a bit to do with Caitlin.

Luke called Delilah over and she came and stood quietly like a good pup. Abigail slipped a ring on Luke's finger and he slipped one on hers. The ceremony ended with their gentle kiss and a standing ovation from the guests. Badger gave his hat to Ryker before taking Hayley's hand and striding over to hug Luke and Abigail. Then he drew Warren aside for a quiet word.

Warren nodded and faced the guests. "Before Hayley and Badger exchange their vows, Badger has something he's composed for Hayley."

Composed? He'd learned how to play the bagpipes in a short time *and* created a tune from scratch? Aaron had always admired the guy's creativity, but this was beyond amazing. His IQ must be through the roof.

Badger fetched the bagpipes from the chair where Ryker had left them. He snapped off a salute to Alec, who sat with his sweetheart Tansy and the rest of the large McGavin clan. Alec grinned and gave him a short, approving nod.

Then Badger turned to Hayley. "There are words to this song, darlin', but I can't play and sing at the same time." He pulled a folded piece of paper out of his pocket. "You'll have to imagine how they go with the music."

She took the paper, her expression stunned. "Badger, I had no idea you wrote a—"

He smiled. "That's the secret for creatin' a great surprise. Here goes." And he began to play. Quietly.

Or at least not as loud as Aaron was used to. He'd heard Alec perform and it wasn't like this. Alec played war pipes that were best listened to outdoors. Badger was making love, not war.

Aaron shifted his position so he could watch Hayley's reaction. She listened with the paper held tight against her heart and her hand pressed to her mouth. Tears glistened in her eyes.

The song ended slowly, with the haunting sound of the pipes fading to a whisper. Badger lowered the instrument and held Hayley's gaze. "I love you."

She tried to speak and failed. Closing the distance between them, she rose on tiptoe and placed a soft kiss on his mouth.

Badger's voice was gruff. "Let's get married, darlin'."

She nodded.

Ryker stepped up, took the pipes and returned them to the chair.

Warren gave his daughter a few moments to compose herself. When he began the ceremony, his voice wasn't completely steady either.

As they faced each other, Badger took his bride's hands in his. Aaron couldn't see Badger's face, but he had a great view of Hayley's. It glowed with a love so deep his chest tightened.

She took a breath. "Dearest Badger, I love you as a partner, a friend, a lover, and, most of all, a playmate." She squeezed his hands and her eyes gleamed.

"Thank you kindly, darlin'."

"Life with you will be crazy, exciting and frustrating, but never dull. I love you when you're brave. I love you when you're kind. I love you when your generous soul shines through. I even love you when you're an idiot."

He ducked his head with a muffled snort of laughter.

"I can't wait to be married to you. And FYI, longevity runs in my family. You'll have to put up with me for a long, long time."

"Throw me in that briar patch, darlin'." Badger squeezed her hands. "My amazin', powerful, stubborn and forgivin' Hayley. The day we met you became my fake fiancée. Didn't take me long to start anglin' for the real deal. Took you a little longer to see things my way. But I kept workin' the program, and here we are, marryin' each other at last."

She swallowed. "Uh-huh."

"I've been told I have the gift of gab. But lookin' at you standin' here today in all your glory, promisin' to be my partner for life...I'm speechless, darlin'." His voice roughened. "I love you so much."

Neither of them spoke and a hush fell, as if no one wanted to break the spell.

At last Warren softly cleared his throat and led them through the rest of the ceremony. Delilah had learned her part and stood quietly as they unfastened the rings from her collar.

The rings went on, Warren blessed their union, and it was done. Badger kissed Hayley with vigor as the guests gave them a standing ovation.

Releasing a blushing Hayley, Badger turned to the gathering. "Time to start partyin'!"

Nicole and Bryce launched into Frankie Ballard's *It's a Helluva Life* and Badger glanced at Warren. "Last ones married, first ones out the door?"

Warren grinned. "Go for it."

Aaron looked around for Caitlin but she'd vacated her spot in the center aisle and was...somewhere else. No telling.

"Need my hat." Badger took it from Ryker and crammed it on his head. "Race you to the champagne, darlin'."

Hayley picked up her skirts. "You're on."

They ran down the aisle as the guests cheered them on.

"We're right behind you!" Luke called out as he grabbed Abigail's hand and whistled for Delilah.

As Luke and Abigail took off with Delilah bounding along behind them, Aaron glanced at Cowboy. "Are we doing that?"

He shrugged. "Can't see why not." He looked across at Wes, Ingrid, Gage and Roxanne. "Let's move 'em out!"

Wes grinned. "Lead the way."

"See you there." Ryker barreled down the aisle with Sheila.

"Let's go." Aaron grabbed April's hand and they ran after them, laughing like kids.

The guests seemed...bemused. Probably hadn't seen anything like this, ever.

Aaron was ready for champagne. And a dance with Caitlin. Time to find out if they had a shot at what Abigail, Luke, Hayley and Badger had found.

22

Nothing like being immersed in a big ol' vat of romance when a girl was attempting to make an objective decision about a very appealing guy. Taking pictures of happy people drunk on champagne, a full moon and love everlasting was Caitlin's current assignment, and she was doing a bang-up job of it.

But all those gooey emotions had gummed up her brain circuits and she was no closer to giving Aaron a definitive answer than she had been twenty-four hours ago. If anything, she was more muddled than ever.

Because of that, she'd dodged and weaved all night to avoid having a conversation with him. Not easy when she was tasked with capturing members of the wedding party either in stills or on video.

She'd chosen to take video of him dancing because he couldn't waylay her then. He was a popular partner, mostly with women at least twice his age. When he waltzed beautifully with Hayley's great-grandmother, those two cleared the floor. He left that sweet lady laughing and fanning herself. Then he asked a little girl about eight, who looked as if she'd won the lottery.

Despite the cool evening, she dashed around so energetically that every thirty minutes or so she had to stop by the bar for a glass of water. That time had come again. She scanned the crowd for Aaron.

There he was, drinking a beer and joking with a group of guys that included Badger and Ryker. Occupied for now. She hurried toward the bar, asked for her glass of water and took her first sip. Checked the group of guys. Wait. Aaron was no longer among them.

"Thought it was about time for your water break."

She turned as he walked toward her, beer bottle in hand, vest unbuttoned. Sometime during the evening he'd ditched the white Stetson. His tousled hair could use a gentle finger-combing. She'd be glad to oblige. "Were you keeping track?"

"Yes, ma'am. You seem determined to avoid me, so I had to strategize." He set his beer on an empty table nearby.

"The thing is—"

His gaze warmed. "Love your dress."

"Thanks." She was a sucker for his low, seductive tone. Raven's voice.

"Will you dance with me? Please?"

Such a sweet request. "I would, but—" She gestured to her camera bag. "I have this."

"I'll bet you could leave it with the bartender."

"You sure can, miss." The bartender was an older guy named Tim who'd come out of retirement to help Virginia with this event. "I'll keep it safe for you. Have a dance. You've been working hard. And he's a good dancer."

"I know." She handed her bag to him. "Thank you. I'll be right back."

"Take your time."

Halfway to the dance floor, Ryker intercepted them, his gaze intent. "Need a word with you, Raven."

"Can it wait until after we—"

"'Fraid not." He tugged down the brim of his Stetson.

A cowboy in a white hat, dispensing justice. Chances were good Ryker had somehow learned about the identity bait-and-switch. She cleared her throat. "If you two need a private chat, I can retrieve my camera and get to work."

Ryker glanced at her. "This concerns you, too. I'd like you to stay, please."

"Sure. What's up?" Like she didn't know.

"Badger let something slip just now. When I questioned him about it, he asked me to let it go. I won't push him on his wedding day, but I get the feeling Badger and Raven have been up to something that involves you. Am I right?"

"Well, I—"

"Yes, we have." Aaron let go of her hand and his sigh of resignation said it all. He was going to confess. "Don't blame Badger, though. He was only trying to help."

"And everything turned out fine." Caitlin moved closer to him, took his hand and gave it a squeeze. "All's well that ends well, as they say."

"Okay." Ryker's jaw tightened but his tone was conversational. "Then I guess you won't mind telling me about it."

"Basically, I caused the problem because I have an issue with—"

"You didn't cause it." Aaron's voice was gentle as he disengaged his hand, squared his shoulders and faced Ryker. "It's unfortunate you caught wind of it tonight, Cowboy. I was planning to fill you in tomorrow."

"Looks like you'll be doing that now."

He grimaced. "Yep." He briefly described the deception, leaving out the more intimate details. He minimized Badger's role and emphasized his own.

As the story unfolded, Ryker's eyes widened in disbelief. Then his gaze darkened and his mouth compressed into a slash of disapproval.

"I finally told Caitlin the truth Thursday night." Aaron glanced at her before returning to Ryker, who looked ready to blow. "She was understandably furious with me and was ready to spread the story around town. Then she talked with Hayley and they voted to keep it to the four of us. Meaning I couldn't tell anyone, including—"

"I get it." Ryker spoke through clenched teeth. "You're damned lucky we're in the middle of a wedding reception, buddy-boy. How could you do something so...so..." He threw up both hands and turned his back, chest heaving. "Honest to God, I feel like punching you."

"I'm not surprised."

Spinning on his heel, he faced Aaron, eyes blazing. "You could have *ruined* this wedding." He jabbed a finger in Aaron's direction. "Caitlin had every right to publicly humiliate you and Badger, but *she* considered the consequences. Which is more than I can say for either of you idiots."

Aaron sucked in a breath. "We..." He exhaled. "You're right. We didn't fully anticipate how it could play out. Things...got out of hand."

"You think?" Ryker clenched and unclenched his fists. "I still can't believe you were willing to trick this wonderful—"

"Ryker." Caitlin stepped forward.

"Ma'am?"

"I'd like to say something."

He frowned. "Look, I don't want you to go easy on them, Caitlin. They don't deserve it. You have a kind and forgiving nature, but what they did—"

"Was wrong. They admit it. But after the truth came out, Aaron said something that stuck with me. He doesn't regret any of it."

"What?"

"And neither do I."

"They set you up! How can you—"

"Because their goal wasn't mean or cruel. They only wanted to show me I could be attracted to Aaron if he called himself something else. And I was. We...had a good time together."

"But now you hate him because he tricked you into liking him, right?"

"I don't hate him. He colored outside the lines to get my attention, but at heart he's a good guy."

"I used to think so, too." He glared at Aaron.

"He *is* a good guy, Ryker. I like him a lot."

"Then you weren't heading to the dance floor just to keep up appearances?"

"No." She looked at Aaron and drank in the warmth shining in his golden eyes. "I'd very much like to dance with him."

"Hm." Ryker's gaze shifted between them. "I still want to punch him for you."

"I appreciate your gallantry, but I'd rather you didn't do that."

"Can't, anyway. I'd likely bloody his nose and he'd drip all over his tux shirt." He turned back to Aaron. "I have more to say to you, soldier, but Caitlin wants to dance with you for some reason or other."

"Can't account for taste."

"That's the God's truth. Think I'll go chew on Badger for a while."

"It's his wedding night."

"I know. I'll make it private, short and to the point. He was the mastermind behind this scheme and don't try to tell me different. It has his fingerprints all over it."

"His heart's in the right place, Cowboy."

"And his head's up his—" He glanced at Caitlin. "Sorry. When I get steamed I sometimes forget myself. If you have any more trouble with this joker, let me know, okay?"

"I will."

"And thank you again for keeping this under your hat. This is Eagles Nest, so the story will get out. But I won't be saying anything."

"Thank you."

"Enjoy your dance." He touched two fingers to the brim of his hat, sent one last scathing glance Aaron's way, and left, his long strides carrying him back to the group that included Badger.

Aaron turned to her, his expression tender. "You defended me. Didn't expect that."

Moving closer, she gave in to temptation and combed her fingers through his hair. "Seems I'm becoming quite fond of you."

He drew her into his arms. "The feeling's mutual."

"Are we going to dance?"

"Sure." He began to sway in time to the music.

Winding her arms around his neck, she nestled against him and followed along. "I meant—"

"I know." His body brushed sensuously against hers. "Some people call this dancing."

"Not you."

He smiled. "Want to go out there?"

"Not especially." She held his gaze, watched the heat build, welcomed the sweet ache of longing. "This is nice."

"Uh-huh."

She stroked his jaw, faintly shadowed by the beginning of his beard. "If you stay much longer, you'll have to duck out and shave."

"No kidding." He rubbed her back in slow, mesmerizing circles. "Thought I'd leave after the brides and grooms take off. How about you?"

"The send-off is the last thing I'll be shooting. Then I'll pack up."

"Wanna come over?"

Her breath caught.

"No pressure. Didn't mean to scare you. Just an idea." His grip tightened slightly. "But I'd love it if you would."

Desire coursed through her, leaving her hot and shaky. "Okay."

_23_

Aaron led the way to his house with Caitlin's Jeep following close behind, her headlights shining in his rearview mirror. The moon was directly overhead, bathing their world in a romantic glow. Perfect timing.

He should have pinned her down about the name thing. They'd agreed on that last night and it was important. But...the invitation had slipped right out.

Not surprising when her warm, supple body had been cradled against his. And he wanted her so much. Maybe this was better—get the hot, urgent stuff under control so they could talk without hyperventilating.

He was battling that very thing as he pulled into his driveway, shut off the engine and exited his truck as if the seat was on fire. A wonder it wasn't, as hot as he was for the woman rounding the front of her Jeep and running, *running* toward him in the moonlight. She'd left her lights on.

The combined velocity as they slammed together nearly sent them tumbling into the piles of leaves at his feet. He managed to gasp out *your lights* before the first kiss happened. He couldn't say who'd started it. He lost track of everything but her mouth...oh, God...her hungry mouth.

He managed to get his hands under her firm bottom and lift her up, crushing her skirt as he pressed her to his throbbing groin. She wrapped her legs around him and sucked on his tongue as he carried her up the steps. Was the door locked?

Wasn't usually, shouldn't be now, but he'd left the house in a hurry and might have reverted to old habits. The knob turned without resistance. He shouldered his way through the door and kicked it shut.

No lights. Didn't matter. Heading for the hallway, he walked directly into his very dark bedroom. He chose the side of the bed where the condoms lived in the nightstand drawer. Lowering her to the soft quilt, he followed her down, drowning in her kisses, aching like he'd never ached before.

She wrenched her mouth from his. "Get the—"

"Yeah." Letting go of her took willpower. Eventually he stood, unbuttoned, unzipped, and yanked open the bedside table drawer. "Take your panties off."

They sailed over his head as he ripped open the package and rolled on the condom. Shrugged off his vest. Left on everything else. Stripping off all his clothes would be great, but he didn't have the time. He'd keep his booted feet on the floor. "Lie back."

"Already did. Come here, you."

He couldn't see a damn thing, but he could feel. He pushed her skirt aside and slid his hands up warm, silken thighs until he encountered wet, hot woman. Bracing one hand beside where her shoulder should be, he used the other to guide him. There.

She gasped as he drove deep. So good he nearly passed out. Gulping for air, he steadied himself. Used both hands to support his weight.

Beneath him, she was breathing hard, too. Her fingers dug into his glutes.

If she kept clutching him to her like the only gift she'd asked Santa for, he wasn't going anywhere. Not that he was complaining. His cock was very happy with its current position. "How're you doing?"

"Never...better."

"Want me to move?"

"Um, yes, please. That would be nice."

"You'll need to loosen your grip."

"Oh." Her fingers relaxed but she kept her hands right where they were and began a slow massage.

Pressure built in his balls. "I could come just from you doing that."

"Should I stop?"

"Only if you want this to last more than sixty seconds."

Her hands stilled. "I just...love touching you."

"We have all night." What a concept.

"We do, don't we?" She sounded fascinated by the idea.

"I'm not going anywhere."

Sliding her hands up his back, she wrapped her arms around him. "Good. I'm staying, too."

Happiness poured through him. She'd been so far out of reach. But now she was here. She was staying.

Leaning down, he estimated from her breathing where her mouth might be. He brushed a tentative kiss in the area and located soft, tasty lips. He nibbled on them. "Since we're both here for the duration, how about if we kick off the evening with a couple of orgasms?"

"That would be lovely."

"Let me know if this works for you." Clamping down on his own hair-trigger response, he initiated an easy rhythm.

Her breathing sped up. "It works."

"I can tell. You're grabbing hold." So easy. So easy when it was right. Filled with the joy of loving her, he gradually increased the pace and rejoiced as she lifted her hips, seeking the pleasure he longed to give her.

Her soft cries spurred him on and he bore down, coaxing her up, up...and over the brink. With a wild cry, she arched beneath him and her hot channel undulated over his thrusting cock.

He came in a rush, plunging into the whirlpool of sensation with her name on his lips. *Caitlin.*

His labored gasps and the buzz in his ears blocked all other sounds. Was this real? Damn well better be. If he woke up alone in his bed...

The haze cleared from his brain. Caitlin lay beneath him, her breathing semi-steady. He cleared his throat. "That was fun."

"Crazy fun." She ran a palm over his chest. "I've never been quite so…spontaneous."

"I think we were ready for that."

She chuckled. "You think so? What was your first clue? Me running across the yard?"

"And leaving your lights on."

"I did?"

"I tried to tell you, but—"

"So they're still on?"

"Far as I know."

She started laughing. "I'll bet my door's standing open, too."

"Come to think of it, I don't remember closing mine."

"We should take care of those things."

"Eventually." He leaned down and allowed himself one more warm, welcoming kiss. She always seemed eager to make that connection, play sexy games with his tongue….

His cock twitched. He lifted his head. "You're not going to believe this."

"Yes, I will."

"But we can't yet."

"I know."

"First I have to—"

"Go out and turn off my lights?"

He placed tiny kisses all over her face. "That's what jumper cables are for."

"You're funny."

"Truthful." He nuzzled behind her ear. "Your battery isn't my priority."

She stroked both hands down his back and cupped his ass. "Mine, either."

"But I'll go out there while I'm up." He eased away from her and stood with one hand on the condom and the other on his pants. Thank God for darkness. Nothing smooth about this pose. "Please make yourself comfortable while I'm gone." He started out of the room since the house was built before attached baths were a thing.

"Is that code for *please take off your clothes*?" she called after him.

He laughed. "Seems to me like you'd be more comfortable making love that way, but suit yourself."

"Lights?"

"By all means." He took care of the condom, washed up and zipped his pants. By the time he walked past his bedroom, the door was closed with a strip of light underneath it. He smiled. She was in there creating some effect or other. He'd bet money on it.

He picked up the pace, striding quickly through the house. He had the urge to start whistling as he walked out on the porch, but that might not be appropriate at one in the morning in his quiet neighborhood. None of his neighbors were up.

The cool night air was welcome on his heated skin. He took the steps two at a time, hurried down the walk and around the front of the Jeep.

Good thing Eagles Nest had the lowest crime rate in Montana. Besides leaving the headlights on and her door open, she'd left her keys in the ignition—an impressive testament to her eagerness for what had just happened.

Their first time. Brief. Intense. He pocketed her keys, switched off the lights and grabbed her purse and camera bag before closing the door.

Hoisting both straps over his shoulder, he jogged around the back of the Jeep and over to his truck. Door was wide open there, too. The headlights turned off automatically or else they'd be on.

During the drive home, he'd fantasized that when she climaxed, she'd call out his name. She hadn't. He jerked his keys from the ignition and shut the door.

Aw, hell, maybe he was putting too big a premium on having her do that. She'd followed him home and thrown herself into his arms. What more did he want?

His cock ached, reminding him of unfinished business in the house. Although the living room and kitchen remained dark, a square of light fell on the grass and leaves in the side yard. His bedroom window.

He'd had to weather turbulence to get to this point. Worth it. Loping across the lawn, he took the steps two at a time, crossed the porch in two strides, and walked in. "Honey, I'm home!"

"Hang on two seconds!"

"That's asking a lot." He set her bag and purse on the table as he counted. "Mississippi one, Mississippi two, I'm on my way." He threw both sets of keys on the table and started on the buttons of his shirt as he headed toward the hall.

The door swung open and hit the doorstop. When he walked in, she made a dive for the bed and scooted under the covers.

"No fair!" He wrenched off his shirt and tossed it on top of the dresser. "I barely saw you."

"That's the idea. Preserve the mystery a little longer."

"I prefer my mystery in books." He leaned against the dresser and pulled off his boots. "With you, I'd rather...."

He paused to look around. Why was the room so pinkish? Ah. She'd found his red bandanas and draped them over the bedside lamps. "I like what you did with the bandanas. Nice effect."

"A little surprise for you. Thanks for turning off the headlights."

"You're welcome." He quickly unbuttoned and unzipped. "I'll bet you look great in that rosy light. Without anything on, hint, hint."

"In a minute." She sat in the middle of the bed hugging the sheet to her breasts. "You first."

"Not much to see here. Standard issue." His gray pants joined the shirt on top of the dresser and he shoved down his briefs.

Her eyes widened. Sucking in a breath, she murmured a soft swear word. "I...uh, knew you were...um, large, but I didn't fully appreciate how..." She swallowed. "Very impressive."

Damn. Now he was blushing. "Thank you, ma'am. Kind of you to say."

"Nothing kind about it, soldier. Just telling it like—"

"Turnabouts fair play," he said gently. "Gonna ditch that sheet for me?"

She slowly lifted her gaze from his package and smiled. "Yes." She threw it aside.

And he lost his mind.

24

Aaron's stunned expression was almost comical. And so sweet. Caitlin soaked up his adoring gaze as it traveled from her bare breasts to her painted toenails and back again, leaving her hot and achy.

He gave her a crooked smile and his chest heaved. "There goes my plan."

"You had a plan?"

"Go slower. Add foreplay." He yanked the bedside table drawer open and glanced at her. "How do you feel about foreplay?"

"Can take it or leave it."

"Good. Let's leave it." He grabbed a condom from the drawer.

"Fine with me." She stretched out on her side. "Watching you suit up that bad boy is all the foreplay I need."

She'd found the perfect sexual partner, a man who was right from the first kiss, the first intimate caress, the first wild coupling. She feasted on the sight of his virile body. She craved the sound of his voice, thick with desire, the musky scent of his arousal, the taste of passion on his tongue.

When he slipped into bed with her, she rolled to her back and held out her arms.

"Ah, my lusty wench." He moved between her thighs. "You want this as much as I do."

"More."

"Debatable." He gazed down at her. "Makes me feel ten feet tall."

"I'm glad you're not." She smiled and wrapped her arms around him. "We'd never fit."

"Yeah, we would. I'd figure it out." He maintained eye contact and probed with the tip of his cock. "Because..." With one quick thrust, he was there, filling her, creating frissons of pleasure. "This."

She gasped. "Yeah."

"I want to go deeper. Wrap your legs around my hips."

She did, hooking her ankles together. She glanced up at him. "Good?"

"Good." He surged forward, squeezed his eyes shut and groaned. "*Very* good."

"Yep." The new position set off delicious shock waves in her core. She shivered in anticipation. Soon.

He opened his eyes. Passion burned hot in their tawny depths as he raked his gaze over her quivering breasts. "So beautiful." His breathing roughened. "Gotta go for it."

"Yes, *please*."

He began to stroke, slowly at first, and then faster, and faster yet.

Her vision blurred and the intensity stole her breath. He hovered protectively above her, the bringer of pleasure, the creator of a climax that edged closer with each rapid thrust. Almost...yes...*now!* She let go with a high, keening cry. He drove home one last time.

Shuddering, he braced himself on his outstretched arms and gulped for air. Murmured something. Then he repeated it again, softly. Her name.

She closed her eyes and savored the aftermath of really great sex.

* * *

The room was silent except for their breathing. Hers was faster than his, more shallow. She liked his easy rhythm better. She adjusted hers to match. Nice. Like dancing.

Opening her eyes, she looked straight into his.

He smiled. "Did you do that on purpose?"

"What?"

"Synchronize your breathing with mine."

"Yeah, I did. I like the way it feels."

"I like the way all of this feels."

"We seem to have hit on something good."

"Yes, ma'am." He leaned down and kissed her gently, no tongue this time. Then he lifted his head to gaze at her. "What next?"

"You know what I'd love?"

"Name it and it's yours."

"Really? Okay, then, a Hasselblad."

"Except that." He picked up a strand of her hair and tickled her cheek. "Try again."

"A shower."

"You can have that, but when you see the setup, you might go for a bath, instead."

"Why?"

"Gorgeous antique claw-foot soaking tub."

"Oh, man, you know how to tempt a girl. Do you use it a lot?"

"No, sad to say. I'm not a soak-in-the-tub kind of guy, so I just shower in it. But I've been told a tub like this is romantic."

"You've been told right. Would we both fit?"

"We will if you're willing to get cozy."

She grinned. "Won't that be hard on you?"

"Well, there's that. But at least you'll be within easy reach so I can get you squeaky clean with the detachable shower head."

The sexy conversation was having a predictable effect on her, which he'd no doubt intended. "Will we have bubbles?"

"I'm not a fan of bubbles."

"Yeah, I suppose they're not manly."

"Not particularly. And they spoil my view."

"I hadn't thought of that." Two could play at this game. "I enjoy a view as much as the next person. I doubt bubbles taste good, either."

His breath caught and the teasing light in his eyes became a speculative gleam. "Sounds like you're ready for a bath."

"So ready."

"Tell you what. I'll take care of a very unromantic chore and start the water. Give me a few minutes before you come down there."

"All right."

"And you should probably grab my bathrobe out of the closet. It's chilly in here."

"I haven't noticed."

"Because you have a hot guy plugged in, keeping you toasty warm. My butt's freezing."

"Really?"

"Not really. Just said it to make you smile. Which you did." He slowly disengaged. "Meet you in the bathroom."

"I used to say that to my girlfriends in junior high when we had problems with the boys."

"And here we are, still giving you problems."

"It's okay. The last hour made up for it."

"Excellent." He left the bed and started out of the room. "That means the next hour should put me solidly in the plus column."

And speaking of solid, he looked almost as good from the back as the front. "Depends how skilled you are with that shower head!" she called after him.

"Very!"

She laughed. This was fun. More fun than she'd had with a guy in...ever. And they hadn't even gotten around to discussing Dick Francis.

Climbing out of bed, she smoothed the rumpled sheets, folded his quilt and laid it across the end of the bed. They wouldn't need it until they went to sleep. If they ever did.

The rumble of water running into a deep tub sounded promising. But he was right about the temperature in the house. Cool enough for a bathrobe.

She located his thick robe, a navy terrycloth with a Badger Air logo patch on it. She slipped it on and was swallowed by soft terry and the scent of his shaving lotion. The hem almost touched her toes.

The lapels created a double layer of terry as she tied the sash, crossed to the door and poked her head out. The water continued to run and flickering light spilled out into the hall. Either the bathroom had caught fire or he'd lit candles.

"Ready for me?"

"Always!"

She laughed and padded barefoot down the smooth wooden floor of the hall. She had to pick up the hem of the robe to keep from tripping. When she arrived, she was rewarded by a camera-worthy moment. He stood with his back to her and a snowy towel wrapped around his hips as he leaned forward, a hand on each of the taps. The shower head hung over the edge of the tub.

Lit votive candles sat on the windowsill and the back of the sink, filling the air with a spicy scent. The warm glow lovingly showcased his broad back, powerful thighs and muscled calves. Photogenic guy.

"Come on in. The level's almost where I want it."

"I like the candles."

He glanced over his shoulder. "Badger showed up early this morning with a box of 'em."

"Why?"

"He wanted me to be prepared, just in case I'd be *needin' some ambiance* as he put it."

"That's...sweet." She stepped onto the cool tile. "I couldn't have admitted this Thursday night, but I'm grateful to the guy."

"You and me, both." He turned off the water and faced her, a grin making his eyes sparkle. "Looks just as cute as I thought it would."

"Generous cut."

"Yeah, I hate skimpy bathrobes. Cowboy and Badger got me an extra-large when I signed on with Badger Air."

"It's a great robe, but I could fit a whole other person in here."

"There's an idea." Reaching out, he hooked his fingers into the sash and urged her closer. "Let's try it." He unfastened the tie and opened the lapels. His breath caught.

"See something you like?"

"Uh-huh." Sliding an arm around her waist, he perched on the edge of the tub and drew her between his spread knees. "Missed out on foreplay." He cupped a breast in each large hand and squeezed gently. "How do you feel about after-play?"

She moaned and closed her eyes. "Love it."

_25_

Soft, silky, fragrant, and delicious. So eager to be loved. Aaron's fantasies of Caitlin paled in the face of reality. Everything about her was just..._more_.

By the time he slipped the robe off and helped her into the tub, she quivered on the edge of a climax. It was a tight fit, especially when he had to work around his very rigid cock. But he managed to cradle her in the curve of his body so he had access to all her special places.

Surrounded by the erotic luxury of warm water and a pulsing spray, she responded by coming...and coming again. Water splashed everywhere. Who cared? He was making Caitlin very happy.

And himself crazy. The swirl of water and the friction of her slick skin had created the perfect storm.

When she came down to earth, would she remember making that sexy comment about the taste of bubbles? If not, he might remind her. He wasn't too proud to beg.

Her breathing gradually slowed and she turned to gaze at him. "You. Are. Amazing."

"Thank you."

"Thank *you*." Her chest heaved. "I'm afraid to look. Did I splash water all over the place?"

"Yeah." He smiled. "Doesn't matter. It's a bathroom. Waterproof."

She glanced up at the windowsill. "Doused a few candles."

"I briefly lost control of the shower head."

"Because I was thrashing around. That was epic."

He combed her wet hair with his fingers. "Glad you had fun."

"Oh, I did." She grabbed the edge of the tub and adjusted her position so she was facing him. Her gaze lowered. Because of all the splashing, his agitated buddy was no longer submerged. "And the fun's not over."

"Oh?" He tried to sound casual but the word came out as a hoarse croak. His cock twitched, more evidence that he was in dire straits.

"I just need to...." Water sloshed as she slid onto her stomach with her feet in the air.

Anticipation squeezed his balls in a vice. He gasped and gripped the sides of the tub as he clamped down on the urge to come. "Need any...um...help?'

"I've got this." Grasping his thighs, she eased forward, sending tiny waves lapping at his family jewels.

He groaned. "God, I hope so."

"Oh, I do. I can't wait to get my hands on you."

"Then..." He gulped in air. "By all means..."

She glanced up through eyelashes spiked with water. "Have fun."

Did he ever. She had sure hands and a mouth that gave him the kind of pleasure that would be seared into his mind and body forever. She took her time loving him, focusing all her attention on his exceedingly lucky cock.

He fought against coming, because something this great deserved to be savored. But he'd been ready to explode when she'd started. So good, though...*ahhh*. He sucked in air through gritted teeth. And lost control.

He came, and came hard, with a bellow worthy of a bull moose. She stayed for the party, taking all he had to give.

When he could breathe, he choked out his gratitude, or what he hoped was gratitude. He might not have made a lick of sense. She'd hijacked his brain.

Slowly she released him and brushed her lips over the damp tip of his cock. "You're welcome." Moving carefully, she rose to her knees, leaned forward and kissed him full on the mouth.

Her kiss was salty. Well, it would be. He cupped the back of her head and took that kiss deeper. With every climax, every moment of surrender, the boundaries between them dissolved a little more. He loved where this was going.

* * *

Drying each other off was almost as much fun as getting wet had been.

Caitlin faced him, her skin rosy and her breathing ragged. "This is crazy. I can't want you again so soon."

"Why not?" He looped the towel around her waist and pulled her warm body close. "Is there a rule about how many times you're allowed to come in one night?"

"Evidently not. But let's...let's see if we can just hang out and talk."

"In the living room? For old time's sake?"

"Sure. We can have a book discussion."

"You've got it." He gave her a quick kiss and released her. "I'll build a fire if you'll be willing to fetch us some McGavin's Pale Ale from the fridge."

"Be glad to." She reached for the bathrobe.

"Cold?"

"Not at all, but if we're going into the living room—"

"We can leave the lights off."

"I'd feel silly sitting naked in those chairs."

"Why?"

"I just would. Maybe because that's where we sat when I came over to see you."

"Hm." She could be onto something. If those chairs represented the past, he sure as hell didn't want to reverse course. Making love in front of the fire was his goal. "How about if I spread the quilt on the floor in front of the fire, instead? Would that feel silly?"

Her eyes gleamed. "Now *that* sounds sexy. I'll get the beer." Handing him the bathrobe, she left the bathroom.

He made tracks for his bedroom and hung up the robe. She'd put her dress on a hanger and hooked it over the closet door. He liked seeing it there, almost as if she'd settled in a bit. Grabbing the quilt from the bed and a condom from the drawer, he headed for the living room.

Light from his bedroom filtered into the hall, allowing him to see well enough to get the fire going. Luckily he'd been looking for mindless chores yesterday, so he'd cleaned out the fireplace and restocked the wood bin.

"Want chips?" Caitlin called from the kitchen.

"Sure!" The logs caught quickly. Sort of like he did whenever he touched Caitlin. Wonder of wonders, she seemed equally combustible when she put her hands on him. He'd never had this much action in a few short hours.

He spread out the quilt and left the condom packet on the small table between the chairs. Didn't want to lose that puppy.

Maybe this should be the last round, though. Before they'd left the reception, she'd told Virginia she'd have some proofs by Monday, which meant she planned to work tomorrow. And he had a flight at twelve hundred hours.

She walked in carrying a tray loaded with their beer, a bowl of chips, and napkins. "Refreshments are served."

"Thanks." He flashed her a grin. "Presentation's great." He took it from her and set it in the middle of the quilt. "I now call the Naked Book Club to order. Have a seat."

She glanced at the condom on the small table and laughed. "That doesn't look like a book to me."

"It's just there in case talking about books gets us all hot and bothered."

"Funny, but that never happens to me when I talk about books."

"But you've never had a book discussion with me."

"That's true." She glanced at the quilt. "Might as well take my usual side." She settled to the left of the tray and picked up her beer and took a sip. "Good stuff. I'm glad I won't have to avoid it anymore."

"I figured that's why you ordered wine last night." He raised his bottle in her direction. "Here's to finding common ground."

She tapped her bottle against his. "That would be a fun code phrase for having sex."

He picked up a chip. "Or making love. It would work for that, too." He popped the chip in his mouth casually, as if he hadn't just thrown down a gauntlet.

Her gaze was hard to read. "I suppose it would." She took another swallow of her beer, set it on the floor at the edge of the quilt and scooped up a handful of chips. "What's your favorite Dick Francis book?"

"That's a tough one. The one you're reading, *Nerve*, would rank in my top ten." And not only because he liked the story. When she'd knocked it off the table, she'd saved him from being a total jerk.

She chewed and swallowed. "Needless to say, I haven't read it yet. How about *Forfeit*? I was fascinated by the tortured hero in that one. I felt sorry for his paralyzed wife, but at the same time—"

"I know. Sad for him. But I wasn't on board with him taking a mistress. In his shoes, I would have made a different choice."

"Like what? Her case was hopeless." She gestured with the beer bottle. "Was he supposed to be celibate for the rest of his life?"

"He could take care of the problem on his own. He doesn't have to—"

"It's not the same level of satisfaction."

"Of course not. But let's say I married you and suddenly you're completely paralyzed, can't make love anymore. While I'm—"

"Young. Virile." Her voice raised in pitch and her skin flushed a lovely pink. "It's not fair that you—"

"But I'm better off than you are. At least I'm capable of sexual release. Not so bad compared to you."

She pinned him with her gaze. "But if I loved you, I'd want more for you than that."

"I admire your selfless attitude, but—"

"And I admire yours! But I would never expect you to suffer to spare my feelings."

"Except it's unkind to the other woman, too. If I loved you, I'd just be having sex with her. She'd never have my heart."

"Oh." She took a shaky breath. "I get your point."

"It's an important distinction."

"I can tell you have strong feelings about it."

"Yes, I do." He put aside his half-finished beer. "And right now, I want to make love to you way more than I want to talk about Dick Francis."

Her attention shifted to his lap and she smiled. "I can tell that, too."

"But that's just me. You may not—"

"Let's table this discussion." She handed him her beer. "I'm getting all hot and bothered."

He grinned. "I can tell." Best book discussion ever.

<u>26</u>

If I loved you...she'd never have my heart. Aaron's words seeped into Caitlin's soul and took up permanent residence. To be loved like that...the conviction in his voice rang true. When he gave his heart to a woman, she would have it forever.

She stretched out on the quilt as he rolled on the condom he'd clearly known they'd use. He came to her with an unhurried certainty this time. Light from the fire played across his face, reflecting in his steady gaze, defining the texture of his dark beard.

He wedged his hips between hers with a familiarity born from all they'd shared. Braced on his forearms, he settled over her, his chest brushing lightly against her breasts. "Just so you know," he murmured, "we're making love. We always have been."

"I knew that."

"Good." He eased his cock into her trembling channel. "Then my motives are clear."

She breathed in as he made the journey to her aching core. Then she exhaled slowly, letting the sensation of being filled wash over her. "You can't misread a guy who goes for broke."

"That's my M.O." Easing back, he slid in tight once again. "And now that I've made it this far, I'm doubling down."

Her breath caught. He'd just let her know that an emotional threshold loomed. She summoned her courage. "Fine with me."

"That's all I need to hear." Lowering his body a fraction more, he made full contact. He settled his chest against hers, giving her just enough of his weight to create an electrifying friction.

Now every thrust delivered shock waves to her core and a delicious body rub. They moved as one, skin to skin, heartbeat to heartbeat. Then he kissed her, joining his breath with hers.

He increased the pace so gradually that her climax took her by surprise. One moment she was immersed in their intense connection. The next, he'd created a dazzling display of fireworks deep within her womb.

Wrenching her mouth from his, she gulped for air. "I didn't...I was..."

"Stay with me." He captured her gaze. "There's more." His golden eyes blazed as he bore down, burying his cock in her quaking body over and over, building the tension higher, ever higher.

He dragged in air. "Now, Caitlin." He pushed deep.

Gasping, she shattered into a million glittering flakes of joy. He was right behind her, shouting in triumph. His massive, shuddering climax vibrated through every cell in her body.

She clung to him as they rode the rolling waves of pleasure in perfect sync. Making love. So much love.

Lying beneath him, matching her breath to his, she drifted in and out of consciousness. His body sheltered her from the cold as the fire burned down to a bed of glowing coals. Peace.

Cool air briefly touched her skin until gentle hands tucked the comforter around her. She dozed until she was jostled partially awake. It seemed he wanted her to move.

"Don't wanna go," she mumbled, her voice thick with sleep.

"Shh." Strong arms lifted her, quilt and all, and carried her into a shadowy room. A bed. A pillow tucked under her head. A warm body cocooning hers. She slept.

* * *

Where the heck was she? Rolling over in semi-panic, she smacked up against a solid wall of muscle.

The source of the muscles grunted in surprise. "Caitlin?"

Aaron's voice. She was in his bed. Pale light filtered through his bedroom window. She gazed into his sleepy eyes. "Sorry. I was disoriented."

"S'okay."

"I need to use the—"

"Take my robe."

"Thanks." She slid out of bed and shivered. She'd accept his offer. Grabbing his robe from the closet, she slipped it on and hiked up the hem as she padded down the hallway. She woke up a little more with each step.

The morning after had arrived. But not just the morning after a casual encounter. This morning after was in all caps.

After taking care of business, she washed up and opened the door. Then she turned back and picked up a bottle of mouthwash sitting on the back of his sink. Pouring a little into the cap, she swished it around and spit it out.

"I'll have some of that, please."

She turned. He stood in the doorway wearing a pair of gray sweats and a t-shirt. His hair was rumpled and his beard had grown in. Looked good on him. Then again, she could be prejudiced.

Her heart swelled with a tender emotion she wasn't ready to name. Her body tingled with one she'd clearly identified—good old-fashioned lust.

His gaze warmed. "Good morning."

"Same to you." She handed him the bottle and cap. "This is serious, isn't it?"

"Sharing a bottle of mouthwash? You bet. Doesn't get any more serious than that." He took a swig, walked over to the sink and spit it out. Capping the bottle, he set it back in its spot and faced her. "Now I'm more kiss-worthy, but there's this to consider." He rubbed a hand over his jaw.

"I don't care." She closed the distance between them and slid her hands up his chest.

"I do." He cupped her face in both hands. "You've already got some whisker burn from last night. Looks like I'll have to start shaving three times a day."

"That sounds serious, too."

"You know it." He brushed his thumbs over her cheeks. "The cost of decent razor blades is getting ridiculous."

"We need to talk."

He sucked in a breath. "I'd like that. But first I need to—"

"Right, right. Is your coffeemaker complicated?"

"Nope."

"Want me to brew us a pot?"

"That would be great. Coffee's in a canister right next to the pot. Grinder's there, too."

"Got it." Rising on tiptoe, she placed a soft kiss on his mouth. "See you soon."

"Help yourself to the leftover pastries from yesterday's breakfast if you're hungry. I'm gonna shave while I'm at it."

"You really don't have to."

"Yes, I really do. I think better after a shave."

She smiled. "If you say so. Me and this ginormous robe will get out of your way." She picked up the hem and walked out into the hall.

On the way to the kitchen, she glanced into the living room, curious as to whether the beer bottles and bowl of chips were still there. Nope.

The kitchen counters were clear, too, except for a plastic-wrapped bakery box. She ground the fragrant coffee beans she found in the canister, filled the reservoir with water and switched on the pot.

She'd noted last night that the kitchen was shipshape, even after six men had cooked and eaten breakfast there yesterday. Not surprising. Three were ex-military, two had been raised by Quinn Sawyer and one by Virginia Bennett.

The wrapped box of pastries called to her. Luke would have brought over a fresh batch and even day-old Pie in the Sky goodies tasted like heaven. She took off the plastic, opened the box and breathed in the aroma. The men had left two cinnamon rolls, a bear claw, three chocolate éclairs and a cheese Danish.

She found a couple of small plates in the cupboard. He'd told her to start eating, but she'd wait. She chose an éclair and debated taking a cinnamon roll, too.

"Ah, go ahead," Aaron said as he walked into the kitchen bringing the scent of shaving cream and lotion with him. "You only live once."

She glanced at him. "I've heard that, but what if it turns out we come around again?"

"Funny you should mention that." He walked over to a cupboard and took out two mugs. "Cheesy as it might sound, I've had that thought about you and me. Like we were lovers in another life." He picked up the coffee carafe. "Want anything in your coffee?"

"Just black, please. Why do you think we knew each other in another life?"

"It would explain why I had such a strong reaction when we met." He poured the coffee. "Do you remember it?"

"I sure do. Ryker introduced me to his buddy Aaron Donahue and I freaked out."

"Yeah, you did." He picked up both steaming mugs and came over to the pastry box. "I'll take one of those eclairs and a cinnamon roll, please, if you'll put them on a plate for me."

"If you don't mind my fingers."

"I love your fingers." He started out of the kitchen. "I'll lick them clean for you if you want."

Heat surged through her. One stray comment and she was ready to ditch the program and go back to his bedroom. She plucked out an éclair for him, gave them each a cinnamon roll and carried the plates out to the dining table. He'd moved her purse and camera bag, hanging both on the coat tree.

He pulled out her chair. "Listen, do you want some scrambled eggs? I just realized I didn't give you the option of something more nutritious. This stuff was available and I—"

"It's fine. Perfect." She set the plates on the table and took the chair he held for her. She gazed up at him. "I can't stay very long, sorry to say."

"I know. I heard you tell Virginia about the proofs." He leaned down. "Thanks for hanging out a little while." He gave her a playful kiss that gradually grew in intensity. "Mmm…" He lifted his head. "You get to me, Caitlin Dempsey."

She smiled and stroked his smooth cheek. "You get to me, too."

He sighed. "But we have places to go and people to see today." He claimed the chair cattycorner from hers. "And plans to make." He looked over at her. "Is that what you meant by *we need to talk*?"

"Sort of." She looked at him. "I feel like we made a commitment last night."

"God, I hope so. I sure did."

"Me, too." She reached over and squeezed his arm. "We have something special. We owe it to ourselves to see where it leads."

He held her gaze. "You're making me a very happy man."

"And you've made me a very happy woman, soldier."

A slight frown came and went. Then he smiled. "I'm not exactly a soldier anymore."

"Oh, I know. It's just a form of endearment, really."

"So you don't have to use my name?" His tone was casual, but his expression was not.

She brushed aside a twinge of uneasiness. "I could use your name. I just—"

"You just don't."

"Sure I do."

He took a deep breath. "No, you don't, Caitlin. Believe me, I would know. I've been listening for it."

"You have? When?"

"When we're talking, when we're in bed together. You called me soldier before we made love the second time. I wasn't going to get into the name thing then, obviously. Convinced myself it didn't matter."

She swallowed. "But it does."

"You were going to tell me during the reception what you'd decided about that, but—"

"I couldn't make up my mind, so when you invited me over, I just said yes."

"Have you made up your mind?"

Her chest tightened. "About you? Yes! You're wonderful! I'd like nothing better than to pursue this relationship."

"That doesn't answer my question."

She dug deep and found the courage to say it. "No matter how much I try, I can't look at you and think *Aaron Donahue*."

"But that's who I—"

"Aaron Donahue is a narcissist. A con man who flattered me into having a sexual relationship with him. Then he cheated on me."

"And I hate that he's such a bastard, but I'm—"

"You're good and kind, a true friend, a generous and funny lover, an all-around amazing person. You're not Aaron Donahue to me."

"Damn." Pushing back his chair, he got up and began pacing the living room.

She ached all over. "I know this isn't what you wanted to hear. What if I called you Raven?"

He shook his head. "My Air Force buddies call me Raven. You're not my pal from the service. You're the woman I—" He coughed. "You're my lover. I want you to call me Aaron."

"I just—"

"I *need* you to call me Aaron." He spun to face her. "It's my effing name, Caitlin. My *name*. A part of who I am. If you can't say it when you look at me, let alone when I'm making love to you, that's a problem. A big one."

"I don't know what to do about it!"

"I don't either, damn it! All I know is I can't fix this. You're the only one who can, and..." He ran his fingers through his hair and stared out the front window. "God, I hate like hell to say this..."

She clenched her hands in her lap, heart pounding, waiting for the ax to fall.

His voice grew hoarse. "We shouldn't see each other anymore until you do." He cleared the emotion from his throat. "If you ever do."

She nodded. "I'll be out of here in five minutes."

27

From heaven to hell. Aaron continued to pace while Caitlin dashed into his bedroom to put on her clothes. He *hated* sending her away. He longed to take it back, apologize, promise to drop the subject. If only he could drop it!

He'd tried ignoring the issue ever since she'd set foot in his house last night. He'd pretended it didn't matter but had secretly waited in vain for that magic moment. When she'd called him *soldier* a second time, he could see that becoming her go-to, a work-around so she'd never have to say his name. Forget that shit.

She'd said she'd be gone in five minutes. She reappeared in four.

He unhooked her purse and camera bag from the coat tree. "Just to warn you, I need to talk this out with someone. Learned that when I was in the hospital."

She met his gaze. Hers was filled with enough pain to last him a lifetime. "By all means." Her voice was toneless, robotic. "Talk to whoever you need."

"The thing is, Badger's on his honeymoon and I don't feel like dealing with Cowboy. I'm going to call Kendra, see if I can come out for a ride soon. I know you're often there for senior pictures, so I—"

"Don't worry about running into me. I didn't make appointments for the first part of this week. I'll be busy with wedding pictures."

"Okay, then."

She took a shaky breath. "I've hurt you and I'm sorrier than I could ever say. I shouldn't have come over here last night."

A knife twisted in his gut. "Don't say that."

"It's true!" She looked away. "I accepted your invitation knowing I hadn't faced the reality of the name problem. I don't know what I expected." Her laugh was bitter. "A miracle transformation in my thinking, I guess."

He closed his eyes. He'd inspired bitterness and recrimination in a woman who was the personification of sunshine and joy. What had he done?

"Instead, every minute I spent with you made it worse." There was a catch in her voice.

He opened his eyes.

Tears glistened in hers. "You're the exact opposite of him. Why do you have to have his name?"

He swallowed a howl of pain. "*Why does he have to have mine?*"

"Well said." She swallowed and reached for the doorknob. "I'll be in touch."

"I'll...focus on that possibility."

"Goodbye..." She took a shaky breath. "Goodbye...Aaron."

She'd choked it out, clearly forced herself to utter those two syllables. Point taken. After she'd closed the door behind her, he hit it hard with his fist. It rattled in the frame. Damn it. Damn it to hell.

* * *

Kendra had an opening to go riding with him on Monday afternoon. Since Kendra was dog-sitting while Luke and Abigail honeymooned in Hawaii, Delilah would tag along on their ride. Suited him just fine. The pup might provide some much-needed comic relief.

Kendra assigned him Jake, as if sensing the smooth-gaited Tennessee Walker was just the horse he needed. She took Licorice to give the mare a break from her rambunctious colt Eclipse. At five months, he was all legs and full of the devil.

Delilah pranced with eagerness as they saddled up. Kendra made small talk about the wedding, although she didn't mention Caitlin. Not once.

Evidently she'd figured out Caitlin was why he was there. He'd mentioned having an issue to discuss, one that was best handled during the ride. She'd likely seen him leave the reception with Caitlin. That had probably set some tongues wagging.

Once they'd gone through the pasture gate, Delilah got busy searching the underbrush for rabbits. The path was wide enough for two horses, which had prompted Kendra to call it the Trail of Secrets. Appropriate.

He turned to her. "Before I start, has Cowboy said anything?"

"Oh, he says things all the time, but he hasn't mentioned you recently. Does he know about this issue you want to discuss?"

"Some of it. Badger had too much champagne Saturday night and some info came to light that shouldn't have. Cowboy asked me to clarify, which I did. He...wasn't happy. Just so you know. I'm not one of his favorites right now."

"Good grief. Ryker loves you. You're the last person I'd expect to be on his bad side. What did you do?"

"Tricked Caitlin into believing I was someone else for three evenings last week."

"What the *hell*?"

"Yeah, I know." And Caitlin had forgiven him. He winced at the injustice of that. She'd forgiven him and he'd held her feet to the fire over the name situation. What a guy.

"Badger came up with that scheme, didn't he?"

"Well, yeah, but I went along with it."

"I *knew* something had happened. Just the way Hayley looked at him when she said *I love you even when you're an idiot* set my antennae vibrating. Sounded like a recent transgression to me."

"He meant well."

"He always does." She sighed. "Okay, son, take it from the top."

He loved that she called him *son*. She didn't mean it literally. Then again, maybe she did. There was a reason he was comfortable laying this problem at her feet. She'd deal with him as if he were her flesh and blood.

Taking a deep breath, he plunged into his narrative. It sounded more ridiculous each time he had to tell the story. How had Caitlin fallen for such a lame performance?

He knew the answer. She had a kind heart. She had romance in her soul and had wanted to believe. The optimist who captured wonder and beauty with her lens had fallen for the tale of a lonely vet.

He glossed over the sexy parts, but Kendra had five grown sons. She'd get the gist.

When he'd finished, she pulled up her horse, nudged back her hat and gazed at him. "What a great plot for a daytime soap opera."

He reined in Jake. "No kidding. It's a damn mess."

"That too. Let me be sure I have everything straight. The plan sort of worked, but in the end, it blew up in your face because she still can't think of you as Aaron Donahue. Is that about the size of it?"

"Yes, ma'am."

"Whew. This is a tough one. I went to school with a kid named Jason. A real snot. Jason is a perfectly fine name and Ian wanted it for one of our sons. I told him no way. I still have a negative reaction when I meet somebody with that name."

His restless gaze settled on the rugged bulk of the mountains. "Yeah, I knew a rotten little girl named Annabelle in fifth grade. Lied, swiped other kids' stuff, bullied the smaller kids. Never did like that name after that."

"What if Caitlin had been named Annabelle?"

He blinked and turned to her. "I never thought of it that way."

"Helps to stand in another person's boots."

"I like to think it wouldn't have mattered, given how much I admire her, but…who knows?" He grimaced. "Maybe it's hopeless, then."

"It's difficult, but not hopeless. Definitely worth it for us to take a shot at Caitlin's prejudice against your name."

"Us? You mean you and me?"

"Oh, sorry. I jumped ahead a few moves. Usually when I say *us* in the context of a campaign, I'm talking about the Whine and Cheese Club."

"A campaign? With those ladies? Hang on, Kendra. I'm not asking you to—"

"You look a little panicked. Don't worry. We won't do anything without your approval."

"Good, because her reaction is totally understandable. More so now that you got me to look at it from her side. I wouldn't want to…to cause her distress."

"You already have."

He groaned. "Okay, then. *More* stress."

She reached over and patted his arm. "Chin up. This is a complicated situation, but we've faced other complicated situations and come out ahead."

"You mean the Whine and Cheese Club."

"I do. Look, we're women and you're not."

He choked on a laugh.

"I realize that sounds like an obvious statement, but our perspective is much different from yours. We're also women of a certain age. Our combined store of wisdom could solve most major world problems if we were given the reins."

"That I do believe, but this is a very delicate—"

"Which is where we shine. First question. Does Caitlin know you're telling me about this?"

"Yes. I told her before she left. Until Saturday night, only the four of us knew—me, Badger, Caitlin and Hayley. Cowboy knows but won't tell anybody. By telling you, I've increased the number to six."

"I want to increase the number to eleven."

"I thought there were only five of you."

"Virginia's a member, now."

"Oh."

"This'll be her first adventure. It'll be good for her to get her feet wet."

"Kendra, I love you and I believe your friends are capable, but that's a lot of folks to be in on this secret. I don't give a damn about myself, but I don't want Caitlin to be embarrassed by town gossip."

"Nothing goes out of our group that shouldn't. We're surgical, quiet and discreet."

"Quiet and discreet? You were on a float in the Fourth of July parade wiggling your asses to *Shake Ya Tailfeather*!"

She laughed. "Discreet when it's called for, outrageous when necessary. Look, nothing will happen if I contact Caitlin and she has no interest in discussing the matter with me. But I have a hunch she'll need to vent, just like you."

"Maybe. Hayley's not here, which leaves her with nobody unless she wants to share the whole mess with someone new. I doubt she does, at least not at this point."

"And you said she doesn't know how to fix this?"

"She doesn't."

"But she'd like to?"

"I think so. I hope so."

"Then if you'll trust me to handle the problem with love and compassion, my friends and I may be able to help."

He hesitated.

"What have you got to lose?"

He laughed and shook his head. "Badger asked me that when I balked at going forward with his plan."

"You just told me you don't regret going through with it, even knowing how snarled up it's become."

"Yeah, the only thing I regret is causing Caitlin pain."

"Like I said, there's a ton of firepower in this group of women. If this can be fixed, we'll fix it."

He drew courage from her confidence. "Okay. Go for it. And holler if you need my help."

"I doubt we will, but I could use it right now."

"Oh?"

"Delilah's found a stick and that means she wants someone to throw it for her. I get tired of throwing it long before she gets tired of chasing it. She's insatiable with that stick routine."

He swung down from the saddle. "Then allow me. I could use a mindless physical task." Then he paused as the light dawned. He looked up at her. "And that's why you asked me to do it."

She smiled. "Throw the stick, son. Throw it hard. After thirty or forty times, you'll feel a whole lot better."

_28_

Desperation drove Caitlin to accept Kendra's offer of an evening of brainstorming with the Whine and Cheese Club on Wednesday night. If Hayley hadn't been in Paris with Badger, she would have been the sympathetic ear Caitlin needed, the friend who could advise her how to navigate her way through this debacle.

But without Hayley, she was in danger of doing something stupid. She almost called her mother. Pouring out the whole miserable story on the phone would accomplish nothing, though. Her parents had only visited Eagles Nest once, right after she moved here, and her mom wouldn't know any of the players. Seemed pointless to drag her into this ridiculous drama.

Two nights in a row she'd picked up her keys with the intent of going over to his house in the wee hours. She missed his strong, loving arms, his laughter, his kiss. Surely they could work this out.

Both times she'd put her keys away because nothing had changed. She'd fallen head over heels for a man with the wrong damn name.

By working like a galley slave, she finished the wedding albums, both physical and digital, on Wednesday afternoon. She ate a quick dinner and made it to the ranch at eight on the dot. Lights glowed in the windows.

She climbed out of the Jeep, her laptop under her arm, and mounted the steps to the front porch. As she crossed the porch and reached for the wrought-iron door knocker, laughter erupted inside the house. If nothing else, these women might help her locate her missing sense of humor.

Kendra opened the door and smiled. "Come on in. Everybody's excited to dig into this problem."

"Um, okay." *Excited? Really?* Bemused by that description, she walked into her first-ever meeting of the Whine and Cheese Club.

"Hey, Caitlin!" Virginia put down her wine and hurried over to give her a hug. "You poor thing. Going through all this in the middle of all the wedding hoopla."

"Yeah, well..." She was saved from having to come up with a response as the other members took turns hugging her and expressing their concern. Got her a little choked up. Made her miss her mom.

"Have a seat, have a seat." Diedre, a curvy woman with curly hair in an eye-popping shade of red, ushered her over to the couch by the fireplace. "I want to see your pictures of him. I have an idea how we can use them."

"We need to get the woman some wine, Deidre." Judy, a short brunette, stood on the other side of the coffee table. "Red or white, Caitlin?"

"Red, please. And thanks."

"I want to see the pictures, too." Christine sat on Caitlin's other side. She was taller and even more willowy than Virginia.

"Me, too." Virginia leaned against the back of the couch.

"I'm not sure how this will help." At Kendra's request, Caitlin had pulled out images of Aaron from the wedding and added them to the ones she'd taken outside his house. She opened her laptop and turned it on. "If I can't think of him as Aaron in person, how can—"

"I'll explain once we're all gathered," Deidre said. "And have refills."

Kendra laughed. "I'll bring out the bottles."

"I've set this up as a slide show." Caitlin called up the file. "Pulled some stills from the video I took at the reception."

"He was a dancing fool at that reception," Deidre said. "I had to quit asking him to dance with me because Jim was getting miffed."

"And when he waltzed with my grandmother," Virginia said, "I just melted."

"Who's ready?" Kendra came in with red in one hand and white in the other.

"All of us," Christine said. "We need fortification for this project."

"Absolutely. Here you go, Caitlin." Judy handed her a goblet.

Kendra glanced around. "Does this remind anybody of that awful kid, Jason?"

"Ugh, yes." Judy made a face. "I still can't stand that name." She turned to Caitlin. "Not sure if you knew Deidre, Kendra, Christine and I were in the same class."

"Yep. Heard that."

"And in the same class with Jason the Jerkoff," Christine said. "He was the worst, Caitlin. Went around snapping our bras, making remarks about our boobs, telling dirty jokes to see if we'd blush."

Judy started laughing. "Then Deidre got fed up and told him he had a classic case of small wienie syndrome. That was a priceless moment. I've never seen a face that red."

"Because I nailed it." Deidre grinned. "The obnoxious ones never have decent-sized schlongs."

"So true." Jo, an elegant woman with short gray hair, saluted Deidre with her wine glass. "I'm glad you put that little twit in his place."

"It was fun."

"I'll bet. Hey, before we get started, I propose a toast. To the friendship of women."

"Perfect." Kendra lifted her glass.

Caitlin glanced around at friendly faces and kind eyes. Whether they helped her solve this problem or not, she was blessed because they were willing to try. She raised her glass. "I'll drink to that."

After everyone had taken a generous sip, Deidre settled back on the couch. "Let the slide show begin."

Caitlin sat quietly as the women exclaimed over the shots. She'd saved the sepia-toned one for last.

"That one." Deidre pointed to the screen. "Oh, God, that'll do the trick."

"Time to reveal your grand plan, Deidre," Kendra said. "Are you going to have her stare at that for two hours a day?"

"Not exactly. But sort of. Caitlin, I want you to project that life-sized on your wall in your apartment. Can you do that?"

"Yes, but—"

"Oh, but before you do, can you Photoshop his name on it? Maybe several times, in different colors and fonts?"

"Guess so."

"Since I'm assuming you'll only have the one projector, we need to pick out some others you can print up and tack everywhere, and I mean *everywhere*, with his name on all of them."

"I'm getting the idea," Christine said. "You want her surrounded night and day with his image."

"His image connected to his name," Jo added. "I think this could work. Total immersion."

"Kind of like brainwashing," Judy said.

"Let's not call it that." Deidre flapped a hand at her. "It has such a pejorative ring to it."

"*Pejorative*." Christine laughed. "Listen to you, showing off your vocabulary. What shall we call it, professor?"

"I know," Kendra said. "Reconditioning."

"Reconditioning." Deidre nodded. "I like it."

"But it won't be enough for her to just look at those images every day," Jo said. "She needs to look at them and say his name. A lot."

"And you know what?" Judy walked around the couch and stood in front of the fireplace, wineglass in hand. "She needs to hear his voice."

"How the heck's she going to do that?" Deidre gestured to the laptop. "Hel-*lo*, these are pictures. No sound."

"I know how." Kendra smiled. "I'll take a video of him and send it to Caitlin. She can put it on her laptop and listen to it several times a day."

Caitlin's head began to spin. "A video of him saying what, exactly?"

"Just one thing," Christine said. "That's more effective in brain—uh—*reconditioning*. I think he should just say something like *Hi, I'm Aaron Donahue.*"

"Or, even better," Kendra said, "*Hi, there, Caitlin. I'm Aaron Donahue.*" She joined Judy in front of the fireplace and gazed at Caitlin. "What do you think?"

"I...I don't know. I guess I could try it. How long would I need to do this?"

"Twenty-one days," Deidre said. "Whenever you're trying to instill a new habit or get rid of an old one, that's the recommended time span."

"So!" Judy bounced on the balls of her feet. "Are you game?"

"I guess so."

"Not strong enough," Deidre said. "Give it more oomph."

"Yes. I'll do it."

"Louder!" Christine said.

"Yes, I'll do it!"

"Ha!" Deidre raised her hand in the air. "We have lift-off! High fives!"

Somewhere in the process of slapping hands with everyone, missing and having to do it over again, Caitlin started laughing. Probably because everyone else was, too.

Eighties music blasted from the stereo unit on the bookshelf. She glanced at Kendra. "What's that for?"

Kendra grinned. "What else? Dancing! You in?"

She grinned back. "Hell, yeah."

* * *

Caitlin had made it through two weeks of the program when Hayley and Badger came home from Paris.

Hayley called her hours after they'd landed. "I'm totally jet-lagged but I have to know. What's going on? Badger got a couple of cryptic texts from Aaron while we were over there."

"Can you come over for a few minutes? You'll understand better if you can see what my apartment looks like."

"I'll be right there." Hayley showed up ten minutes later.

Caitlin led her upstairs.

Standing in the middle of the living room, she turned in a slow circle, her eyes wide. "What *is* this?"

"My reconditioning program." She filled her in on the evening with the Whine and Cheese Club. "Oh, and there's more." She gestured to her laptop sitting open on her desk. "Have a seat. I watch this several times a day." She clicked on the video of Aaron.

He leaned casually against a sleek plane sporting the Badger Air logo. Then he straightened, stepped closer and smiled. "Hi, there, Caitlin. I'm Aaron Donahue." The video ended.

Hayley looked up at her. "That's damned effective. If I weren't madly in love with Badger, I'd want to date him. So smart of whoever made the video to take it out at the airfield."

"Kendra. She went there the next day and talked him into letting her take it. She made him do it over until she'd decided he looked dreamy enough."

"Well, he looks super dreamy to me." She stood. "I assume you have more pictures in your bedroom."

"And my bathroom and kitchen nook. He's everywhere."

"And you have a week to go."

"Yep."

"What do you think? Is it working?"

She took a deep breath. "It's making me incredibly horny."

"I'll bet. But what about the name situation."

"It's way easier to say now that I have to repeat it a hundred times a day. I dream about him constantly, too. In my dreams, I say his name straight to his face, no problem. But when I finally see him again, face-to-face..." She shrugged. "That'll be the test."

"Have you set something up?"

"The Whine and Cheese ladies advised me not to communicate directly with him until the three weeks are over. I sent a message through Kendra that I'd like to meet him at his house a week from tonight, although I couldn't make any promises I'd be *reconditioned*. He said okay."

"Do you think you will be? Reconditioned, I mean."

"God, I hope so, Hayley. I miss him so much it isn't funny."

"I'll bet he's in the same boat."

"That's why I'm doing this." She gestured around the room. "We deserve a shot and like he said two weeks ago, I'm the only one who can give us one."

29

Almost time, and Aaron was ready to chew nails. If everything went south, Badger was poised to charge to the rescue with beer and crude comedy videos. He'd called twenty minutes ago to extract a solemn promise Aaron would text him and not try to tough it out alone.

Caitlin's Jeep pulled up in front of his house on the dot. He'd wanted her to be early. Not her style, though. Not his either, usually.

He stayed in the house although every muscle in his body strained with the urge to open that door and run down the walkway. He had to keep it together, though.

Three weeks had been like three lifetimes. Once he got his arms around her, no telling if he could control himself. He was liable to make love to her in the front yard. Before they talked. Before he had any idea if her self-imposed program had worked. Then they could be right back where they started.

So he gripped the back of the easy chair to anchor himself in place. When she rang the doorbell, he didn't move. "It's open!"

She stepped inside wearing the soft blue sweater and jeans she'd had on the first time she'd come to see him. He didn't think that was an accident. She wanted to start over.

Her gaze found his. The connection clicked into place. He held his breath.

"Hello, Aaron." She said it without hesitation.

So far, so good. "Hello, Caitlin. Missed you." His heart beat so fast it made the front of his shirt quiver.

"I've missed you, too." She took a shaky breath. "Although I've seen a lot of you these past three weeks."

"Must be sick of me by now."

"On the contrary." She took a step closer. "Those three weeks were precious to me because I—well, I learned something very important."

"That you can say my name and not hate the sound of it?" *Please, oh, please let that be true.*

"I can. I've talked to you for three solid weeks. I've greeted you every morning and bid you good night before I went to bed."

His breathing quickened. She was working up to something. He could see it in her eyes and the flush on her cheeks.

"This morning, I said words to you that I hadn't ever said before. They sounded right."

"What..." He cleared his throat. "What did you say?"

"I love you, Aaron Donahue."

He exploded into action, crossing the room in three strides, groaning with relief as he pulled her into his arms. "I love you, Caitlin Dempsey."

She gazed up at him, her eyes luminous. "I thought you might, Aaron Donahue."

He grinned. "Keep it up. Sounds dorky as hell. I don't give a damn. Keep saying it."

"Aaron Donahue, Aaron Donahue, Aaron Donahue, Aaron Dona—"

He kissed her. Sweet heaven, she was back in his arms, kissing him like there was no tomorrow. Except now they had tomorrow, and the next day, and the day after that. Tomorrows stretched as far as his heart could see.

Cupping his face in both hands, she put a millimeter of space between her mouth and his. "And now I have a request."

"Anything."

"Make love to me, Aaron Donahue, so I can shout your name to the world."

Epilogue

Nothing more aerobic than chasing after a couple of six-month old foals. Seth Turner and his buddy Matt had been at it for about fifteen minutes. Both dams grazed near the pasture gate, clearly ready for a warm stall in the Buckskin Ranch's spacious barn, a hay flake and some oats. But these two hooligans wanted to play keep-away.

Harry, a black and white Paint, was more docile than Hermione, a roan filly. Matt almost had the colt a couple of times, but Hermione's mad dash to the far side of the pasture was a siren's call to Harry. Seth had assigned himself to the filly, and so far, she was winning this contest, hoofs down.

Matt stood, hands on his hips, watching the pair cavort in the Montana twilight. "I've never seen them so full of it."

"It's the weather. Just enough coolness in the air to get their blood pumping."

"Thanks to them, so's mine."

"Ah, it's good for your heart. Besides, we won't have evenings like this much longer. I don't care if this takes a while, do you?"

Matt shrugged. "Not really. Rather not miss dinner, though."

"Then let's double-team Harry. If we get him, she won't want to stay out here alone."

"Good thinking."

"You go left and I'll go right. Act casual, like you don't care if you catch him or not."

"You been reading those horse psychology books again?"

"I'm telling you, it helps me deal with these critters."

"If you say so, Dr. Freud." Matt sauntered off. "Here I go, minding my own business. Don't give a damn if I catch me a colt or not. Just out for a stroll."

Seth grinned. "Great job. But nudge back your hat. Your body language says you're relaxed but your hat's tugged down like you're on a mission."

"Oh, for God's sake." He thumbed back his hat and kept walking. "Is my jacket the right style? I'd hate to mess this up because my jacket sends the wrong message."

"It's fine." While moving parallel to Matt, he kept an eye on Harry, who'd stopped to graze. "They're used to seeing that jacket. But I don't wear buffalo plaid much anymore, especially if I don't know the horse."

"You're kidding."

"A solid color's more calming than a bold pattern. At least that's what I've seen."

"I get plenty of compliments from the ladies when I wear this jacket."

"I'm sure you do, lover-boy."

"You should come out with us Saturday night. Have some beers. Dance with some pretty girls."

"I'll think about it."

"That's what you always say. And then you don't. I know it's been tough. Everybody gets that, but—"

"I'll definitely think about it." Hermione had trotted to the far corner of the pasture, attitude sticking out all over her. Harry continued to graze as if he couldn't care less about them. But his ears flicked back and forth. He was listening, evaluating.

"You do that. And while you're at it, think about coming on the ski trip over Christmas. Cowboys on skis. Gotta love it."

"Sounds like fun." He drew within a yard of Harry. "Don't make any sudden moves, but if he dodges your way, see if you can get a grip on his halter."

"Will do."

"Hey, Harry." He spoke in an easy, conversational tone. "How about heading back to see Mom, kiddo?"

The colt lifted his head and gazed at him, his jaw still working on the tidbits of grass he'd managed to find.

"Grass is just about done for the season, sport. More tasty stuff in the barn. Just sayin'." He slowly reached for the halter. The soft crackle of hooves on dry grass told him Hermione was in the vicinity. "Where's the filly?"

"Coming up right behind you."

"Then maybe you should get Harry, I'll see if I can sweet-talk that little girl into cooperating."

"Go for it."

"Hermione, your timing's excellent." He pivoted slowly. "Harry says he's ready to get cozy in the barn. Doesn't that sound nice? Have some dinner, cuddle with your mama?"

She tossed her head.

Matt huffed out a breath. "Got Harry."

"And I've almost got this filly. We're just negotiating. Aren't we, sweetie?" He leaned toward her and reached for her halter. "That's it. Stay right—"

With a loud snort, she wheeled and took off. He grabbed a handful of air, lost his footing and ended up on his butt. "That didn't go exactly as planned."

Matt cracked up. "No?" Keeping a grip on Harry, he led the foal over and gave Seth a hand up. "Looked perfect to me."

He laughed and dusted off his jeans. "That's what I get for thinking I know what I'm doing."

"Hard to outsmart a rambunctious filly." Matt held his gaze. "It's good to hear that laugh again, buddy. Missed it. Guaranteed you'd do a lot more of it on this ski trip."

"Hmm." He set off after Hermione. Matt could be right. A ski trip would be fun, but he had other fish to fry.

When his mom had died suddenly a year ago, he'd been responsible for...everything. No siblings, no other living relatives. He'd given away her clothes, sold her furniture and shoved her more personal items into boxes. Last month he'd found the courage to sort through that stuff and he'd found a thirty-year-old diary.

And learned the truth about his dad. She'd always refused to talk about him except to say they'd loved each other desperately and losing him had been devastating. Any questions about how and when he'd died had gone unanswered. Too painful. Couldn't even speak his name.

He had a name, now—Hamish McGavin.

They'd dated for about a year when she'd lived in Bozeman. His dad and his dad's younger brother Ian had lived with their parents on a sheep farm near a small town called Eagles Nest. When his grandparents had decided to sell out and return to Scotland, Ian had stayed to marry a woman named Kendra. His dad had moved to Scotland.

His mom *had* been devastated, for sure, but her diary entries made it clear she hadn't wanted to live in Scotland any more than his dad had wanted to stay in Montana. Maybe he was dead. Maybe he wasn't. Maybe it didn't matter because she'd never tried to contact him about the pregnancy.

At first he'd been pissed and hurt that she'd misled him. But eventually he'd looked at the situation from the viewpoint of a young woman who wanted to keep the whole thing under wraps and build a life for her son. He could see it.

But now, the wrappings were coming off. The internet had yielded plenty of info on Eagles

Nest and it was chock full of McGavins. Chances were good he was related to at least some of them.

His plans hadn't crystalized, but he wouldn't be going on the ski trip. When his Christmas break started, he'd be on the road to Eagles Nest.

Wrangler Seth Turner's captivated by mom-to-be Zoe Bradford. Too bad she's not looking for a baby daddy! It'll be a Christmas they'll never forget in A COWBOY'S HOMECOMING, the final book in the McGavin Brothers series!

* * * * *

"I'd love to hear about training foals." Zoe picked up a fry. "These days I'm fascinated with babies of all kinds. You might have some tips for me."

"I doubt that training a foal is—"

"They're newborns, too."

"With hooves and teeth."

She laughed. "There's that. But I'd be interested in your process. I'll bet there are commonalities."

"Okay." He scooped up his burger. "First off, I make sure I'm there for the birth and that I have plenty of chances to touch the foal. That creates a bond." He took a generous bite.

"See? Touch is universal." And dancing with him had made her keenly aware that she hadn't been touched a whole lot in the past few months. The full body contact he'd created by pulling her close at the end of the dance had filled a yearning she hadn't acknowledged.

He put down his burger and started in on his fries. "The foals love it. If their first experience with humans is the pleasure of being stroked and fondled, they're so much easier to work with."

Whoa. This wasn't an academic discussion of raising young creatures. Instead he was using words like *stroked* and *fondled.* She should change the subject. She didn't want to. "Tell me more."

He warmed to his subject, and *warmed* was the operative word. His enthusiasm for his work shone in his eyes and vibrated in his voice. Clearly he loved his job, which evidently was very hands-on.

She figured he was good with his hands. Even the way he ate, corralling his burger neatly without dropping any of the contents, demonstrated that. She'd learned when they'd danced that his hands were work-roughened, a new experience for a city girl.

She'd never made love with a man who had callouses at the base of his fingers. How would it feel? But she had no business thinking about Seth in that way. Or any other man. Cutting her mental vacay short, she concentrated on her juicy burger and crisp, salty fries.

When they'd finished the meal, he glanced at her empty plate and his. "Do you want dessert?"

"No, thanks. I'm stuffed. You go ahead if you want."

"None for me." He looked over at the stage, where Bryce and Nicole strummed the opening chords of the next number. "Let's have one more dance before we leave."

She was ridiculously happy that he'd asked. Probably another bad sign. She should say no. But... "I'd like that."

New York Times bestselling author Vicki Lewis Thompson's love affair with cowboys started with the Lone Ranger, continued through Maverick, and took a turn south of the border with Zorro. She views cowboys as the Western version of knights in shining armor, rugged men who value honor, honesty and hard work. Fortunately for her, she lives in the Arizona desert, where broad-shouldered, lean-hipped cowboys abound. Blessed with such an abundance of inspiration, she only hopes that she can do them justice.

For more information about this prolific author, visit her website and sign up for her newsletter. She loves connecting with readers.

VickiLewisThompson.com

www.ingramcontent.com/pod-product-compliance
Lightning Source LLC
LaVergne TN
LVHW040614250326
834688LV00035B/552